Retold Classics

NOVELS

Frankenstein

Huckleberry Finn

The Red Badge
of Courage

The Scarlet Letter

A Tale of Two Cities

Treasure Island

ANTHOLOGIES

American Classics,
Volume 1

American Classics,
Volume 2

American Classics,
Volume 3

American Classics,
Nonfiction

American Hauntings

British Classics

Classic Chillers

Edgar Allan Poe

Jack London

Mark Twain

World Classics

The Retold Tales® Series features novels, short story
anthologies, and collections of myths and folktales.

Perfection Learning®

ABOUT THE AUTHORS

PAT PERRIN

Wim Coleman and Pat Perrin are a husband-and-wife writing team. Their adult books include *PragMagic, Jamois Vu Papers,* and *Terminal Games*. They have also written a seven-book series for young adults called *The Decryptors Science Fiction Series*. Besides books, Coleman and Perrin have created their own newsletter and written articles and essays.

In addition to writing, the two have worked individually as a teacher, editor, playwright, technical writer, visual artist, waiter, pizza cook, and horse breeder. Coleman has a B.F.A. in Theater Arts and an M.A.T. in English and Education from Drake University. Perrin has a B.A. in English from Duke University, an M.A. in liberal studies from Hollins College, and a Ph.D. in art theory and criticism from the University of Georgia.

WIM COLEMAN

ABOUT THE ARTIST

Sue Cornelison is a freelance illustrator and designer. She works in various media including oil, acrylic, colored pencil combined with mineral spirits, pastels, watercolors, and gouache.

SUE CORNELISON

She most enjoys illustrating books for children, but she also illustrates posters, cookbooks, greeting cards, and craft designs. She likes the challenge of having a wide variety of projects.

In addition to freelancing, Cornelison has worked as a high school art teacher and tumbling coach in her rural town of St. Charles, Iowa. When not working, she enjoys spending time with her husband and four children.

Retold Classics

Chillers

by Wim Coleman and Pat Perrin

Perfection Learning®

Senior Editor

Marsha James

Editors

Lisa Owens
Lisa Morlock

**Cover and Inside
Illustration**

Sue Cornelison

Book Design

Sue Bjork

For information contact
Perfection Learning® Corporation
1000 North Second Avenue, P.O. Box 500
Logan, Iowa 51546-0500
Phone: 1-800-831-4190 • Fax: 1-800-543-2745
perfectionlearning.com

PB ISBN-10: 0-7891-1895-5 ISBN-13: 978-0-7891-1895-0
RLB ISBN-10: 0-7807-6576-1 ISBN-13: 978-0-7807-6576-4

14 15 16 17 PP 13 12 11 10

TABLE
OF CONTENTS

WELCOME

WELCOME TO THE RETOLD CLASSIC CHILLERS

A killer ferret, grave robbers, ghost sightings, and the living dead. What do these things have in common? They're all a part of the frightening and intriguing stories collected for *Retold Classic Chillers*.

We call something a classic when it is so valued that it is saved and passed down to new generations. These classic stories have been around for a long time, but they're not dusty or out of date. That's because they can be brought back to life by each person who reads and enjoys them.

The *Retold Classic Chillers* are stories written to engage and frighten readers years ago, before Stephen King, Anne Rice, and Christopher Pike. And still they continue to shock and entertain us today.

RETOLD UPDATE

This book presents a collection of eight adapted classics. All the vivid and terrifying details of the original stories are here. But longer sentences and paragraphs in the stories have been split up. And some old words have been replaced with modern language.

In addition, a word list has been added at the beginning of each story to make reading easier. Each word defined on that list is printed in dark type within the story. If you forget a word while you're reading, just check the list to review the definition.

You'll also see footnotes at the bottom of some story pages. These notes identify people or places, explain ideas, or help you pronounce the words and phrases.

Finally, at the end of each tale you'll find information about the author and background on the story. These revealing and interesting facts will give you insight into the writer's life and work.

When you read the *Retold Classic Chillers*, you bring each haunting story back to life in today's world. We hope you'll discover why these tales, written by masters of the language, have earned the right to be called classics.

DRACULA'S GUEST

BRAM STOKER

VOCABULARY PREVIEW

Below is a list of words that appear in the story. Read the
list and get to know the words before you start the story.

anxiety—uneasiness; nervousness
appealingly—beggingly; in a pleading way
bleak—bare; gloomy
comparative—near; close
custom—tradition; practice
depart—leave; go away
desolation—emptiness; gloominess
despair—misery; hopelessness
foundations—bases or supports of a building
glistening—dazzling; sparkling
instinct—sense or feeling; impulse
ironically—in a mocking or teasing way
paralyze—stun; make powerless
phantoms—ghosts; spirits
picturesque—interesting; attractive
protest—objection; complaint
straggling—stray; random
tedious—dull and lengthy; tiresome
tempest—violent storm
uncanny—unreal; astonishing

Dracula's Guest

Jonathan Harker is an English businessman on his way to Transylvania for a meeting with a certain Count Dracula. What's expected to be an uneventful trip turns into a strange and mysterious adventure.

As we prepared for our drive, the sun was shining brightly on Munich.[1] The air was full of the joy of early summer. Herr Delbrück was the *maître d'hôtel*[2] of the *Quatre Saisons,*[3] where I was staying. Just as we were about to **depart**, he came down to the carriage. He wished me a pleasant drive, but he kept holding on to the handle of the carriage door.

"Remember, you must be back by nightfall," he said to Johann, the coachman. "The sky looks bright. But there is a shiver in the north wind. That means there may be a sudden storm. But I am sure you will not be late." He smiled and added, "For you know what night it is."

Johann answered with a forceful, *"Ja, mein Herr!"*[4]

Touching his hat, Johann drove off quickly. When we had cleared the town, I signaled for him to stop.

[1]Munich is a city in Southwest Germany.
[2]A *maître d'hôtel* is French for "master of the hotel."
[3]*Quatre Saisons,* French for "four seasons," is the name of the hotel.
[4]*Ja, mein Herr* is German for "yes, sir."

"Tell me, Johann," I said, "what is tonight?"

He crossed himself[5] and answered bluntly, *"Walpurgisnacht."*[6]

Then he took out his silver watch. It was an old-fashioned German watch as big as a turnip. He looked at it with a frown and gave a little impatient shrug of his shoulders. I realized that this was his way of politely complaining about the unnecessary delay.

I sank back in the carriage and motioned for him to go on. He started off rapidly, as if to make up for lost time. I noticed that every now and then, the horses seemed to throw up their heads and sniff the air uneasily. Whenever that happened, I looked around in alarm.

The road was **bleak**. We were crossing a rather high, wind-swept plateau.[7] As we drove, I saw what appeared to be a little-used road that dipped through a small winding valley. It looked very pleasant there. At the risk of offending Johann, I called him to a stop.

When he had pulled up, I told him I would like to drive down that road. He made all sorts of excuses and kept crossing himself. This stirred my curiosity, so I asked him many questions. He answered as though fencing[8] and repeatedly looked at his watch in **protest**.

Finally, I said, "Well, Johann, I want to go down this road. I shall not ask you to come unless you like. But tell me why you do not want to go—that is all I ask."

For his answer, he jumped from the box. He reached the ground so quickly that he must have thrown himself from his seat. Then he stretched out his hands **appealingly** and begged me not to go.

There was just enough English mixed with his German for me to understand most of what he said. He always seemed just about to tell me something—the very idea of which seemed to frighten him. But each time he paused, crossed himself, and said, *"Walpurgisnacht!"*

[5]To cross oneself is a sign of religious devotion.
[6]*Walpurgisnacht* is the eve of May Day, or May 1st. The English call it Walpurgis Night.
[7]A plateau is an area of level, high ground.
[8]In the sport of fencing, one dodges to avoid the opponent's weapon.

I tried to argue with him. But it was difficult to argue with a man when I did not know his language. He certainly had the better of me because of that. He began to speak in broken English. But he kept getting very excited and breaking into his native tongue. Every time he did so, he looked at his watch.

The horses became restless and sniffed at the air again. At this, Johann grew very pale and looked around in a frightened way. Suddenly he jumped forward, took the horses by the bridles, and led them on some twenty feet.

I followed and asked why he had done this. For an answer, he crossed himself. He pointed to the spot we had left. Then he drew the carriage in the direction of the other road, pointing to where the roads crossed.

He said, first in German and then in English, "Buried him—him—what killed themselves."

I remembered the old **custom** of burying people at crossroads who had committed suicide. "Ah, I see, a suicide. How interesting!" But, for the life of me, I could not make out why the horses were so frightened.

While we were talking, we heard a sort of sound between a yelp and a bark. It sounded far off, but the horses got very nervous. It took Johann a long time to quiet them. He was pale, and he said, "It sounds like a wolf. But yet there are no wolves here now."

"No?" I said, questioning him. "Hasn't it been a long time since the wolves were so near the city?"

"Long, long," he anwered, "in the spring and summer. With this snow, the wolves couldn't have been here long."

He petted the horses and tried to quiet them. Dark clouds drifted rapidly across the sky. The sunshine passed away. A breath of cold wind drifted past us. It was only a breath, however, and seemed more like a warning than a real wind. Then the sun came out brightly again. Johann looked under his lifted hand at the horizon.

"The storm of snow, he comes before long time," he said. Then he looked at his watch again. He held the reins firmly, for the horses were still pawing the ground restlessly and shaking their heads. He climbed quickly to his seat as though the time had come for continuing our journey.

I felt a little stubborn and did not get into the carriage at once.

"Tell me," I said, "about this place where the road leads."

He crossed himself again and mumbled a prayer before he answered, "It is unholy."

"What is unholy?" I inquired.

"The village."

"Then there is a village?"

"No, no. No one has lived there for hundreds of years."

This stirred my curiosity. "But you said there was a village."

"There was."

"Where is it now?"

At that, he burst into a long story in both German and English. The languages were so mixed up that I could not understand exactly what he said. But I understood that hundreds of years ago, people had died there. They had been buried in the ground. Later, sounds were heard under the clay. When the graves were opened, men and women were found rosy with life, their mouths red with blood.

Of course, those who still lived there were in a hurry to save their own lives. So they fled to other places. They fled to where the living lived and the dead were dead and not—not—! (He seemed afraid to speak the last words.)

As Johann went on with his story, he grew more and more excited. It seemed as if his imagination had taken hold. He ended in a perfect fit of fear—white-faced, sweating, trembling, and looking around him fearfully. He seemed to expect that something dreadful would show itself there in the bright sunshine on the open plain. Finally, in complete **despair** and agony, he cried, *"Walpurgisnacht!"*

He pointed to the carriage for me to get in. My English blood rose at this. Standing back, I said, "You are afraid, Johann—you are afraid. Go home. I shall return alone. The walk will do me good."

The carriage door was open. I took from the seat my oak walking stick, which I always carry on my travels. I closed the door. Pointing back to Munich, I said, "Go home, Johann. *Walpurgisnacht* doesn't worry Englishmen."

The horses were now more restless than ever, and Johann was trying to hold them in. Excitedly, he begged me not to do anything so foolish. I pitied the poor fellow. He was deeply serious, but I could not help laughing.

His English was quite gone now. In his **anxiety,** Johann had forgotten that his only means of making me understand was to talk my language. He jabbered away in his native German. It became a little **tedious.** After ordering Johann to go home, I turned to take the cross-road into the valley.

With a hopeless gesture, Johann turned his horses toward Munich. I leaned on my stick and looked after him. He went slowly along the road for a while. Then a tall, thin man came over the hill. I could see that much in the distance.

When the man drew near the horses, they began to jump and kick about. They screamed with terror. Johann could not hold them in. They bolted down the road, running away madly. I watched them go out of sight and looked again for the stranger. But I found that he, too, was gone.

With a light heart, I turned down the side road. It went into the deepening valley that Johann had feared. As far as I could tell, there was not the slightest reason for him to feel so. I suppose I tramped for a couple of hours without thinking of time or distance. Certainly, I did not see a person or a house.

So far as the place was concerned, it was **desolation** itself. But I did not much notice this until I turned a bend in the road and came upon an area that was scattered with trees. It was then that I recognized my mood had been much changed by the desolation of the region.

I sat down to rest myself and began to look around. It struck me that it was much colder than it had been at the beginning of my walk. There seemed to be a sort of sighing sound around me. Now and then, from high overhead, came a sort of muffled roar.

I noticed thick clouds drifting rapidly across the sky. There were signs of a coming storm in some high layer of the air. I was a little chilly. Thinking it was from sitting still, I started my journey again.

The land I traveled on now was much more **picturesque.** There were no striking objects that the eye might single out. But in all there was a charm of beauty.

I took little notice of time until the deepening twilight forced itself upon me. Then I began to think of how I would find my way home now that the brightness of the day had gone. The air was cold, and the drifting clouds high overhead were more visible. They were joined by a faraway rushing sound. And I seemed to hear, at times, the mysterious cry that the driver had said came from a wolf.

I waited for a while. I had said I would see the deserted village, so I went on. I soon came upon a wide stretch of open country that was enclosed in hills all around. The hillsides were covered with trees that spread down to the plain. The trees dotted the gentler slopes that appeared here and there. I followed the winding of the road with my eye. I saw that it curved close to one of the thickest clumps of trees and was lost behind it.

As I looked, there came a cold shiver in the air, and the snow began to fall. I thought of the miles and miles of bleak country I had passed. Then I hurried to seek the shelter of the wood before me. The sky grew darker and darker. The snow fell faster and heavier. The earth before and around me became a **glistening** white carpet. And the further edge was lost in misty vagueness.

The road was here, but it was rough. In a little while, I found that I must have strayed from it. For I suddenly missed having the hard surface underfoot, and my feet sank deeper in the grass and moss.

Then the wind grew stronger and blew with increasing force. I was happy to run before it. The air became icy cold, and despite my exertion, I began to suffer.

The snow was falling thickly. It whirled around me in such rapid swirls that I could hardly keep my eyes open. The heavens were torn to pieces by bursts of lightning. In the flashes, I could see a great mass of trees ahead of me, chiefly yew and cypress. They were all heavily covered with snow.

Soon I was in the shelter of the trees. In the **comparative** silence, I could hear the rush of the wind overhead, and the blackness of the storm blended into the darkness of the night. The storm seemed to be passing away. It now came in isolated fierce puffs or blasts. At such moments, the weird sound of the wolf was echoed by many similar sounds around me.

Now and again, a **straggling** ray of moonlight came through the black mass of drifting cloud. It lit up the area. I saw that I was at the edge of the thick mass of trees. And, as the snow ceased to fall, I walked out from the shelter. I began to look around more closely.

I had passed many old **foundations**. It seemed to me that among them a house might still be standing. But I figured I could find some sort of shelter, even in ruins, for a while. As I skirted around the wooded area, I found that a low wall encircled it. Following this, I presently found an opening.

Here the cypresses formed an alley leading up to a square mass. It was some kind of building. Just as I caught sight of this, however, the drifting clouds hid the moon. I passed up the path in darkness. The wind must have grown colder. I shivered as I walked. But there was hope of shelter, so I soldiered on.

I stopped, for there was a sudden stillness. The storm had passed. Perhaps echoing nature's silence, my heart ceased to beat for a moment. Suddenly, the moonlight broke through the clouds and showed me that I was in a graveyard. The square object before me was a massive tomb of marble. The tomb was as white as the snow that lay on and all around it.

With the moonlight came a fierce sigh of the storm. The blizzard resumed its course with a long, low howl. It sounded like many dogs or wolves. I was awed and shocked.

I felt the cold steadily grow upon me until it gripped me by the heart. The flood of moonlight still fell on the marble tomb, but the storm gave further signs of renewing.

Driven by some sort of fascination, I approached the tomb to see what it was. I wondered why such a thing stood alone in such a place. I walked around it and read in German:

COUNTESS DOLINGEN OF GRATZ
IN STYRIA
SOUGHT AND FOUND DEATH
1801

The structure was made up of a few vast blocks of stone. On top of the tomb was a great iron spike or stake. It seemed to be driven through solid marble. Carved in great Russian letters was this saying: "The dead travel fast."

There was something **uncanny** about the whole thing. It gave me a turn and made me feel quite faint. I began to wish, for the first time, that I had taken Johann's advice. Then a thought struck me in a most mysterious way and with a terrible shock. This was Walpurgis Night!

Walpurgis Night was when, according to the beliefs of millions of people, the devil was afoot. It was when the graves opened and the dead came forth and walked. It was when all evil things of earth and air and water celebrated.

This was the very place the driver had specifically stayed away from. This was the deserted village of centuries ago. This was where the suicides lay. And this was the place where I was alone and weak.

I was shivering in a cloud of snow with another wild storm gathering over me! I needed all of my beliefs—all the religion I had been taught. It took all of my courage not to give way to an attack of fright.

And now, a perfect tornado burst upon me. The ground shook as though thousands of horses thundered across it. This time, the storm brought hailstones that beat down leaf and branch. They made the shelter of cypresses of no more use than if their stems were standing corn.

I rushed to the nearest tree, but I was soon glad to leave it. I sought the only spot that seemed to offer shelter, the deep doorway of the marble tomb. I crouched against the massive bronze door, where I gained a certain amount of protection from the onslaught of hailstones. Now they only drove against me whenever they bounced off the ground or the side of the marble.

As I leaned against the door, it moved slightly and opened inward. The shelter of even a tomb was welcome in that cruel **tempest.** I was about to enter when a flash of forked lightning lit up the whole of the heavens.

My eyes were turned toward the darkness of the tomb. In that instant, as I am a living man, I saw a beautiful woman. She had rounded cheeks and red lips. And she was seemingly sleeping on a bier.[9]

As the thunder broke overhead, I was grasped as if by the hand of a giant and hurled out into the storm. The whole thing was sudden. Before I could feel the shock, moral as well as physical, I felt the hailstones beating me down. At the same time, I had a powerful feeling that I was not alone.

I looked toward the tomb. Just then came another

---

[9]A bier is a stand or platform on which a corpse or coffin is placed.

blinding flash. It seemed to strike the iron stake on top of the tomb and pour through to the earth. The blast crumbled the marble with a burst of flame. The dead woman rose for a moment of agony while she was caught in the flame. Her bitter scream of pain was drowned in the thunder crash.

The last thing I heard was this mingling of dreadful sound. Again I was seized by the giant grasp and dragged away. Brutal hailstones hit me, and the air echoed with the howling of wolves.

The last sight that I remembered was a vague, white, moving mass. It was as if all the graves around me had sent out the **phantoms** of their sheeted dead. They were closing in on me through the white cloudiness of the driving hail.

Eventually, I came back to my senses. Then I felt a dreadful sense of weariness. For a time I remembered nothing, but my awareness slowly returned. My feet were in terrible pain, yet I could not move them. They seemed to be numb.

There was an icy feeling at the back of my neck and all down my spine. My ears, like my feet, were dead—yet they were in pain. But there was a sense of warmth in my breast that was, by comparison, delicious. It was a nightmare—a physical nightmare, if one may use such an expression. For some heavy weight on my chest made it difficult for me to breathe.

This period of tiredness seemed to last a long time. As it faded away, I must have slept or fainted. Then came a sort of disgust, like the first stage of seasickness. I had a wild desire to be free from something—I knew not what. A vast stillness surrounded me, as though the whole world was asleep or dead. The silence was only broken by a low panting that sounded as though some animal was close to me.

I felt a warm rasping at my throat. Then I became

aware of the awful truth. It chilled me to my heart and sent the blood surging up through my brain. Some great animal was lying on me and licking my throat. I feared to stir, for some **instinct** told me to lie still.

But the brute seemed to realize that there was some change in me. It raised its head. I saw above me the two flaming eyes of a gigantic wolf. Sharp, white teeth gleamed in its red, gaping mouth. I could feel its hot breath upon me.

I remembered no more for another spell of time. Then I became aware of a low growl, followed by a yelp. This pattern was repeated again and again.

Then I heard a faraway "Hello! Hello!" that sounded like many voices calling in unison. I raised my head cautiously. I looked in the direction from which the sound came, but the cemetery blocked my view. The wolf continued its strange yelping.

A red glare began to move around the grove of cypresses, as though following the sound. As the voices drew closer, the wolf yelped faster and louder. I was afraid to make either sound or motion.

The red glow came nearer. It shone over the white gloom that stretched into the darkness around me. Then all at once from beyond the trees appeared a troop of horsemen. They came at a trot, and they were bearing torches. I could tell that they were soldiers by their caps and long military cloaks.

The wolf rose from my breast and headed toward the cemetery. I saw one of the horsemen raise his carbine[10] and take aim. Another horseman aimed, and I heard the ball whiz over my head. He had evidently mistaken me for the wolf.

Another soldier sighted and shot the animal as it tried to slink away. Then the troop rode forward at a gallop. Some came toward me. Others followed the wolf as it disappeared among the snow-clad cypresses.

I tried to move as they drew nearer. Although I could

[10]A carbine is a lightweight rifle with a short barrel.

14

see and hear all that went on around me, I was powerless. Two or three of the soldiers jumped from their horses and knelt beside me. One of them raised my head and placed his hand over my heart.

"Good news, men!" he cried. "His heart still beats!"

Someone poured a little brandy down my throat. It put some life back into me. I was able to fully open my eyes and look around. Lights and shadows were moving among the trees, and I heard men call to one another. They drew together, whispering in frightened voices. The lights flashed as the others came pouring out of the cemetery. They rode recklessly, like men gone mad.

The further riders came close to us. Those who were already nearby asked them eagerly, "Well, have you found him?"

The reply rang out hurriedly, "No! No! Come away quick—quick! This is no place to stay, and on this of all nights!"

"What was it?" The question was asked in many tones of voice. Many different and unclear answers came. It seemed as though the men were moved by some common wish to speak. Yet they were held back from saying their thoughts by some common fear.

"It—it—indeed!" jabbered one. His wits had plainly given out for the moment.

"A wolf—and yet not a wolf!" shouted another.

"No use trying for him without the sacred bullet," a third remarked in a more ordinary manner.

"It serves us right for coming out on this night! We have truly earned our thousand marks!"[11] were the outcries of a fourth.

"There was blood on the broken marble," said another after a pause. "The lightning never brought that there. And for him—is he safe? Look at his throat! See, men, the wolf has been lying on him and keeping his blood warm."

The officer looked at my throat and replied, "He is all

[11]A mark is a unit of German money.

15

right. The skin is not pierced. What does it all mean? If the wolf had not been yelping, we would never have found this fellow."

"What became of it?" asked the man who was holding up my head. He seemed the least panic-stricken of the party. His hands were steady. On his sleeve was the chevron[12] of a low-ranking officer.

"It went to its home," answered the other, whose long face was pale. He actually shook with terror as he glanced around him. "There are enough graves there in which it may lie. Come, men—come quickly! Let us leave this cursed spot."

The officer raised me to a sitting position as he uttered a word of command. Then several men placed me upon a horse. He sprang to the saddle behind me and took me in his arms. He gave the word to go forward. Turning our faces away from the cypresses, we rode away in swift, military order.

As yet my tongue refused its job, and I was helplessly silent. I must have fallen asleep. The next thing I remembered was finding myself standing up. I was supported by a soldier on each side of me. It was almost broad daylight.

To the north, a red streak of sunlight was reflected in the waste of snow. It made a path like blood. The officer was telling the men to say nothing of what they had seen. He told them to say that they had found an English stranger, guarded by a large dog.

"Dog! That was no dog," cut in the man who had shown such fear. "I think I know a wolf when I see one."

The young officer answered calmly, "I said a dog."

"Dog!" repeated the other **ironically**. It was evident that his courage was rising with the sun. Pointing to me, he said, "Look at his throat. Is that the work of a dog, master?"

Instinctively, I raised my hand to my throat. As I touched it, I cried out in pain. The men crowded around to look, some stooping from their saddles.

And again came the calm voice of the young officer.

[12]A chevron is a V-shaped badge or insignia worn on the sleeve of a military uniform to indicate rank.

"A dog, as I said. If anything else were said, we would only be laughed at."

I was then mounted behind a trooper, and we rode on into the suburbs of Munich. We came across a stray carriage into which I was lifted. It was driven off to the *Quatre Saisons.* The young officer rode along with me, and a trooper followed with his horse. The others rode off to their barracks.[13]

When we arrived, Herr Delbrück rushed quickly down the steps to meet me. It was apparent that he had been watching from within. Taking me by both hands, he carefully led me in. The officer saluted me and was turning to withdraw. When I saw that he was about to leave, I insisted that he come to my rooms.

Over a glass of wine, I warmly thanked him and his brave horsemen for saving me. He replied simply that he was more than glad. He said that Herr Delbrück had already taken steps to please everyone in the searching party. At that vague statement, the *maître d'hôtel* smiled. Then the officer said that he had work to do and left.

"But Herr Delbrück," I inquired, "how and why was it that the soldiers searched for me?"

He shrugged his shoulders as if to belittle his own deed. He replied, "I was lucky. I got permission to ask for volunteers from the commander of the regiment[14] in which I served."

"But how did you know I was lost?" I asked.

"The driver came here with the remains of his carriage. It had been upset when the horses ran away."

"But surely you would not send a search party of soldiers merely because of that?"

"Oh, no!" he answered. "But before the coachman arrived, I had this telegram from the Boyar[15] whose guest you are." And he took from his pocket a telegram. He handed it to me, and I read:

---

[13]Barracks are housing units for soldiers.
[14]A regiment is a unit of soldiers.
[15]A Boyar is a member of the higher Russian nobility.

BISTRITZ.[16]

BE CAREFUL OF MY
GUEST—HIS SAFETY IS MOST
PRECIOUS TO ME. SHOULD
ANYTHING HAPPEN TO HIM,
OR IF HE BE MISSED, SPARE
NOTHING TO FIND HIM. PRO-
TECT HIS SAFETY. HE IS
ENGLISH AND THEREFORE
ADVENTUROUS. THERE ARE
OFTEN DANGERS FROM
SNOW AND WOLVES AT
NIGHT. LOSE NOT A
MOMENT IF YOU SUSPECT
HARM TO HIM. I ANSWER
YOUR CARE WITH MY
WEALTH.

DRACULA

As I held the telegram in my hand, the room whirled around me. If the watchful *maître d'hôtel* had not caught me, I would have fallen. There was something so strange in all this, something strange and impossible to imagine. There grew on me a sense of my being in some way the sport of two opposing forces.

The mere idea seemed to **paralyze** me. I was certainly under some form of mysterious protection. From a distant country, a message had come. It was a message that took me out of the danger of sleep and the jaws of the wolf. And it had come in the very nick of time.

[16]Bistritz is a town in Transylvania.

INSIGHTS INTO
BRAM STOKER   *(1847–1912)*

The story "Dracula's Guest" does not appear in Bram Stoker's novel *Dracula*. He omitted it because the book was too lengthy. After his death, his widow, Florence, published it with some of his other stories.

Although there have been many films and stage versions of *Dracula*, none is likely to ever capture the terror of the novel. This is partly because *Dracula* is written in the form of the letters and diaries of its characters. "Dracula's Guest," for example, comes from Jonathan Harker's diary. This method makes the events of *Dracula* seem frighteningly real. We really witness the story through the eyes of the characters.

Stoker modeled the character of Dracula on an actual historical figure, Vlad V (1456–1476), who was also known as Dracula. Vlad was an Eastern European prince. Though surely not a vampire, Vlad was known for committing acts of terrible torture and cruelty. There is an actual Castle Dracula in modern-day Romania.

In addition to his writing, Stoker worked as manager for Henry Irving, a famous actor of the time. Stoker himself became famous as soon as *Dracula* was published. And people have been reading and talking about *Dracula* ever since.

Other works by Bram Stoker:
Dracula, novel
Dracula's Guest, short story collection
The Lair of the White Worm, novel

SREDNI VASHTAR

SAKI

VOCABULARY PREVIEW

Below is a list of words that appear in the story. Read the list and get to know the words before you start the story.

arid—extremely dry
chanted—sang
cult—followers; believers
defiantly—boldly; in opposition
disagreeable—unpleasant
exercised—practiced; observed
guardian—one who is legally responsible for the care of another person
haven—shelter; safe place
hoard—collection; supply
lull—pause; break
professional—trained; knowledgeable
represented—served as an example for; symbolized
respectable—honorable; worthy
rite—custom; ceremony; ritual
shrill—loud; piercing; high-pitched
shrine—sacred place that honors a holy person or event
spasms—outbursts; eruptions
spur—encouragement; prompting
stationed—placed; positioned
triumph—succeed; win

Sredni Vashtar

Conradin is a sickly boy with a wild imagination. He even invents his own god with great powers. At first Conradin believes these powers are imaginary—until his most horrifying wish comes true.

Conradin was ten years old. The doctor had given his **professional** opinion that the boy would not live another five years. The doctor was of weak character and counted for little. But Mrs. De Ropp agreed with him completely. And *she* counted for nearly everything.

Mrs. De Ropp was Conradin's cousin and **guardian.** In his eyes, she **represented** three-fifths of the world's people—the three-fifths that were necessary and **disagreeable** and real. Conradin belonged to the other two-fifths—the two-fifths that were always fighting against the first. He kept that part deep inside his imagination.

One of these days, Conradin supposed, he would give in to Mrs. De Ropp's powerful pressures. He would become weary and accept her tiresome diagnosis of his illness, her strict rules, and her drawn-out dullness. Without his imagination, he would have given in long ago. His thoughts went wild under the **spur** of his loneliness.

Mrs. De Ropp would never have admitted to herself that she disliked Conradin. Not even in her most honest moments would she do that. She always defeated his wishes "for his good."

Conradin hated her fiercely, but he was perfectly able to mask it. The few pleasures he could invent for himself gave him great joy. His happiness grew whenever it seemed likely that his invented pleasures would displease his guardian, who was completely locked out of his imagined world.

Conradin found little to attract him in the dull, cheerless garden. Too many windows overlooked it—windows that were always ready to open with a message not to do this or that.

The few fruit trees in the garden were set carefully out of his reach. The blooms seemed to be rare examples of their kind in this **arid** waste. No market-gardener would have offered ten shillings[1] for their entire yearly crop.

In a forgotten corner of the garden, however, was an unused toolshed of decent size. It was almost hidden behind a dismal bush. Conradin found a **haven** within its walls. To him, the toolshed could be a playroom or a cathedral.

He had populated the toolshed with many familiar phantoms. He called them forth, partly from history and partly from his own brain. But the shed also boasted two inmates of flesh and blood. In one corner lived a ragged-feathered Houdan hen.[2] The boy heaped affection on the hen, for his feelings had hardly any other outlet.

Further back in the gloom stood a large cage. It was divided into sections. One of the sections was fronted with iron bars close together. This was the home of a large ferret. A friendly butcher boy had once smuggled it, cage and all, into the toolshed. Conradin had bought it in exchange for a long-hidden **hoard** of small silver.

Conradin was dreadfully afraid of the graceful, sharp-fanged beast. But it was his most treasured possession. Its very presence in the toolshed was a secret joy. He carefully kept it from the knowledge of the Woman. (That was what he privately called his cousin.)

And one day he created a wonderful name for the beast. He called it Sredni Vashtar. Heaven knows how he came up with this name. But from that moment, the ferret grew into a god and a religion.

The Woman **exercised** her religion once a week at a nearby church. She took Conradin with her. But to him,

[1] A shilling is a British coin of small value; it is no longer in use.
[2] A Houdan is a breed of chicken named after a village in France.

the church service was like a strange **rite** in the House of Rimmon.[3]

Every Thursday Conradin went into the dim, musty silence of the toolshed. There he worshipped before the wooden cage where Sredni Vashtar lived. The boy held mystical and complicated rites for the great ferret. When in season, red flowers were offered at the ferret's **shrine.** Scarlet berries were offered in the wintertime. For Sredni Vashtar was a god. And this god laid special importance on the fierce, impatient side of things. This was unlike the Woman's religion. As far as Conradin could see, hers went to great lengths in the other direction.

During great festivals, powdered nutmeg was scattered in front of the ferret's cage. It was essential to the offering that the nutmeg be stolen. These festivals occurred from time to time and were usually devoted to some passing occasion.

On one such occasion, Mrs. De Ropp suffered from a sharp toothache for three days. Conradin kept up the festival during the entire three days. He almost managed to persuade himself that Sredni Vashtar had caused the toothache. If the pain had lasted for another day, the nutmeg supply would have been used up.

The Houdan hen was never drawn into the **cult** of Sredni Vashtar. Conradin had long ago decided that she was an Anabaptist.[4] He did not pretend to have the least knowledge as to what an Anabaptist was. But he privately hoped that it was daring and not very **respectable.** Mrs. De Ropp was the model on which he based his view of respectability. And Conradin hated all respectability.

After a while, Conradin's interest in the toolshed began to attract his guardian's notice.

"It is not good for him to be fooling around down there in all weather," she quickly decided.

At breakfast one morning, she announced that the Houdan hen had been sold. It had been taken away

[3]Rimmon is a pagan god mentioned in the Bible (2 Kings 5:18).
[4]An Anabaptist was a member of a 16th-century radical group that participated in the Reformation of the Catholic church.

overnight. She peered at Conradin with her short-sighted eyes. She was hoping for an outbreak of rage and sorrow. She was even ready to scold him with a flow of excellent lessons and reasoning.

But Conradin said nothing. There was nothing to be said. Something perhaps in his determined face gave her a moment of uncertainty.

At tea that afternoon, there was toast on the table. It was a treat that she usually banned. She claimed that it was bad for him and that the making of it "gave trouble." That was a deadly misdeed in her middle-class feminine eye.

She saw that he did not touch it.

"I thought you liked toast!" she exclaimed with a hurt look.

"Sometimes," said Conradin.

In the shed that evening, there was a change in the worship of the cage-god. Conradin usually **chanted** his praises. Tonight he asked a favor.

"Do one thing for me, Sredni Vashtar."

The thing was not named. Since Sredni Vashtar was a god, surely he was supposed to know what Conradin wished for. Conradin choked back a sob as he looked at that other empty corner. Then he went back to the world he so hated. And every night, in the welcome darkness of his bedroom, Conradin's bitter prayer went up. And every evening, in the dusk of the toolshed, he prayed again.

"Do one thing for me, Sredni Vashtar."

Mrs. De Ropp noticed that the visits to the shed did not stop. So one day, she went to the shed herself.

"What are you keeping in that locked cage?" she asked. "I bet it's guinea pigs. I'll have them all cleared away."

Conradin shut his lips tight. But the Woman searched his bedroom until she found the hidden key. Then she marched down to the shed to complete her discovery.

It was a cold afternoon, and Conradin had been ordered to stay in the house. He **stationed** himself at the far window of the dining room. From there, the door of the shed could just be seen beyond the corner of the shrubbery.

He saw the Woman enter. He imagined her opening the door of the sacred cage. She was peering down with her short-sighted eyes into the thick straw bed where his god lay hidden. Perhaps she would poke at the straw in her clumsy impatience.

Conradin passionately breathed his prayer for the last time. But as he prayed, he knew that he did not believe. He knew that the Woman would soon come out with that pinched smile on her face—the very smile he hated so much. Then, in an hour or two, the gardener would carry away his wonderful god. It would no longer be a god. It would simply be a brown ferret in a cage.

He knew that the Woman would **triumph** now as she always triumphed. He knew that he would grow ever more sickly under her pestering. He would grow weaker under her greater and more powerful wisdom. Then one day, nothing would matter much with him. And the doctor would be proved right.

Conradin felt the sting and misery of his defeat. He began to chant the hymn of his threatened idol loudly and **defiantly:**

Sredni Vashtar went forth.

His thoughts were red thoughts, and his teeth were white.

His enemies called for peace, but he brought them death.

Sredni Vashtar the Beautiful.

Suddenly, he stopped his chanting. He drew closer to the window. The door of the shed still stood ajar. The minutes slipped by. They were long minutes.

He watched the starlings[5] running and flying in little groups across the lawn. He counted them over and over again. But he kept one eye on the swinging door.

[5]A starling is a bird with speckled feathers.

A sour-faced maid came in to lay the table for tea while Conradin stood and waited and watched. Hope crept by inches into his heart. Now a look of triumph began to blaze in his eyes. Before now, those eyes had only known the sad patience of defeat.

Under his breath, he resumed the chant of victory and destruction. He sang it with a secret joy. And soon his eyes were rewarded.

Out through that doorway came a long, low, yellow-and-brown beast. Its eyes were a-blink at the fading daylight. The fur of its jaws and throat was covered with a dark, wet stain. Conradin dropped to his knees.

The great ferret made its way to a small brook at the foot of the garden. It drank for a moment. Then it crossed a little plank bridge and was lost to sight in the bushes. Such was the passing of Sredni Vashtar.

"Tea is ready," said the sour-faced maid. "Where is the mistress?"

"She went down to the shed some time ago," said Conradin.

The maid went to summon her mistress to tea. While she did, Conradin fished a toasting fork out of the sideboard.[6] He began to toast himself a piece of bread. While the bread toasted, Conradin listened. He buttered his toast with much butter. And during the slow enjoyment of eating it, he listened again.

Noises and silences came in quick **spasms** beyond the dining room door. He heard the loud, foolish screaming of the maid. Cries from the kitchen area answered. Then came scrambling footsteps. Someone was hastily sent for outside help.

After a **lull,** there were frightened sobbings. Then there was the shuffling tread of those who bore a heavy weight into the house.

"Whoever will break it to the poor child? I couldn't for the life of me!" cried a **shrill** voice.

While the others argued the matter among themselves, Conradin made himself another piece of toast.

[6]A sideboard is a piece of dining room furniture with drawers and shelves.

INSIGHTS INTO SAKI

(1870–1916)

"**S**aki" was the pen name of Hector Hugh Munro, a British author who mostly wrote short stories. He seems to have taken this name from a long Persian poem entitled *The Rubáiyát of Omar Khayyám.*

Not all of Saki's stories deal with horror or the supernatural. Many are humorous, witty, and satirical. But in a way, most of them are about monsters of a sort. These monsters are ordinary human beings.

Saki was born in the southeast Asian country of Burma to an upper-class British family. After the death of his mother, he was raised by two aunts who gave him little kindness and affection.

This greatly affected his view of human beings. Even his humorous stories are often about how cruel and thoughtless people can be to each other—especially wealthy adults. "Sredni Vashtar" is a typical Saki story—it shows a child getting revenge on the adult world.

In addition to his many stories, Saki wrote a historical book entitled *The Rise of the Russian Empire.* He made his living mostly as a journalist, working in countries all over the world. He did a great deal of military service despite his generally poor health.

The story of his death is like something out of one of his stories. He was serving as a soldier in France during World War I. One dark morning in a trench, he was heard saying to another soldier, "Put that bloody cigarette out." Those were his last words. He was killed by a sniper a few moments later.

Other works by Saki:
"Gabriel-Ernest," short story
"The Music on the Hill," short story
"The Open Window," short story
The Unbearable Bassington, novel
"The Unrest Cure," short story
The Watched Pot, play

THE CASK OF AMONTILLADO

EDGAR ALLAN POE

VOCABULARY PREVIEW

Below is a list of words that appear in the story. Read the list and get to know the words before you start the story.

avenged—revenged; repaid
cask—wine barrel
consulting—asking; seeking advice from
descended—climbed down
excessive—extreme; too much
explicit—clear; specific
feeble—dim; weak
grope—blindly search
grotesque—odd; freakish
ignoramus—fool
impose—take advantage of; intrude
interior—inner; inside
intoxication—drunkenness
leer—grin or smirk; sly look
motto—saying; slogan
prided—took pride in; congratulated oneself
recesses—depths
recoiling—jumping back
retribution—punishment; repayment
vigorously—forcefully; with energy

THE CASK OF AMONTILLADO

● ● ● ● ● ● ● ● ● ● ● ● ●

"No one insults me without punishment" is the Montresor family motto. How seriously does young Montresor take this motto? An unlucky nobleman named Fortunato is about to find out.

Over the years, I had stood the thousand wrongs of Fortunato as I best could. But when he insulted me, I vowed revenge. However, you know the nature of my soul well. You will not think that I uttered a threat. *Sooner or later,* I would be **avenged**—this was a point definitely settled. But the very certainty with which it was decided ruled out the idea of risk.

I must not only punish, but punish without being punished myself. A wrong is not paid back when **retribution** overtakes its avenger. It is also unpaid when the avenger fails to make himself known to him who has done the wrong.

It must be understood that neither by word nor deed had I given myself away. Fortunato had no cause to doubt my goodwill. I continued, as usual, to smile in his face. He did not see that my smile now was at the thought of his destruction.

He had a weak point—this Fortunato—although in other ways, he was a man to be respected and even feared. He **prided** himself on being an expert in wine. Few Italians have the true spirit of genius at this. For the most part, their enjoyment of wine is merely suited to the time and opportunity. Their purpose is to trick British and Austrian millionaires.

In paintings and the study of gems, Fortunato, like his countrymen, was a quack.[1] But in the matter of old wines, he was the real thing. And in this way, I did not differ from him very much. I knew about Italian wines myself and bought them whenever I could.

It was about dusk one evening during the greatest madness of Carnival.[2] I met my friend. He approached me with **excessive** warmth, for he had been drinking much.

The man wore the costume of a jester.[3] He had on a tight-fitting striped dress. On top of his head was a pointed cap and bells. I was so pleased to see him that I thought I should never finish wringing his hand.

I said to him, "My dear Fortunato, I'm so lucky to meet you! How remarkably well you look today! I have received a **cask** of what passes for Amontillado.[4] And I have my doubts about whether it truly is Amontillado or not."

"How?" asked Fortunato. "Amontillado? A cask? Impossible! And in the middle of Carnival!"

"As I said, I have my doubts," I replied. "And I was silly enough to pay the full Amontillado price without **consulting** you. You were not to be found, and I was fearful of losing a bargain."

"Amontillado!"

"I have my doubts."

"Amontillado!"

"And I must satisfy them."

"Amontillado!"

---

[1]A quack is someone who falsely passes himself or herself off as an expert.
[2]In Italy, Carnival is a celebration with lots of costumes, dancing, food, and drink.
[3]A jester is a costumed clown or comedian who usually performs for kings or nobility.
[4]Amontillado is a Spanish wine.

"Since you are busy, I am on my way to see Luchesi. If anyone knows his wines, it is he. He will tell me—"

"Luchesi cannot tell Amontillado from Sherry."

"And yet some fools would say that his taste is a match for your own."

"Come, let us go."

"Where?"

"To your vaults."[5]

"My friend, no. I will not **impose** upon your good nature. I know you are on your way to meet someone. Luchesi—"

"I am meeting no one. Come."

"My friend, no. It is not that. But I see that you are suffering in the severe cold. The vaults are unbearably damp. They are encrusted with nitre."[6]

"Let us go, nevertheless. The cold is nothing. Amontillado!"

Thus speaking, Fortunato took my arm. I put on a mask of black silk and drew a cloak close around me. He hurried me to my palazzo.[7]

There were no servants at home. They had run away to make merry in honor of the holiday. I had told them that I should not return until the morning. And I had given them **explicit** orders not to stir from the house. These orders were enough, I knew, to ensure their disappearance. They were gone, one and all, as soon as my back was turned.

I took two torches from their holders and gave one to Fortunato. I guided him through several groups of rooms to the archway that led to the vault. I passed down a long and winding staircase, warning him to be careful as he followed. We finally came to the bottom of our climb. We stood together on the damp ground of the catacombs[8] that belonged to my family, the Montresors.

My friend's step was unsteady, and the bells upon his cap jingled as he walked.

[5]A vault is a room with arched walls and ceiling, often underground.
[6]Nitre is sodium nitrate; the presence of nitre on the walls of the vaults shows that the walls are extremely damp.
[7]A palazzo is a large house.
[8]Catacombs are underground tunnels often used for burying the dead.

32

"The cask?" he asked.

"It is farther on," I said. "But see the white web-work that gleams from these cavern walls."

He turned toward me and looked into my eyes. His misty eyes dribbled the tears of **intoxication.**

"Nitre?" he asked, at length.

"Nitre," I replied. "How long have you had that cough?"

"Ugh! ugh! ugh!—ugh! ugh! ugh!—ugh! ugh! ugh!—ugh! ugh! ugh!—ugh! ugh! ugh!"

My poor friend found it impossible to reply for many minutes.

"It is nothing," he said at last.

"Come," I said with decision. "We will go back. Your health is precious. You are rich, respected, admired, beloved. You are happy, as I once was. You are a man to be missed. For me it is no matter. We will go back. You will be ill, and I cannot be to blame. Besides, there is Luchesi—"

"Enough," he said. "The cough is nothing. It will not kill me. I shall not die of a cough."

"True—true," I replied. "And indeed I did not mean to alarm you unnecessarily. But you should use proper caution. A drink of this Medoc[9] will defend us from the damps."

At this point, I drew a bottle from a long row of its fellows. I knocked off the neck of the bottle.

"Drink," I said, giving him the wine.

He raised it to his lips with a **leer.** He paused and nodded to me in a chummy way while his bells jingled.

"I drink," he said, "to the buried that rest around us."

"And I drink to your long life," I replied.

He took my arm again, and we went on.

"These vaults are very large," he noticed.

"The Montresors were a great and large family."

"I forget your coat of arms."[10]

"A huge human foot of gold on a field of blue. The foot crushes a raging serpent, whose fangs are imbedded in the heel."

---

[9] Medoc is a red wine from the Bordeaux region of France.
[10] A coat of arms is a family seal or emblem.

"And your **motto?**"

"Nemo me impune lacessit."[11]

"Good!" he said.

The wine sparkled in his eyes, and the bells jingled on his head. My own imagination grew warm with the Medoc. We had passed through walls of piled bones mixed with large and small casks. We reached the inner **recesses** of the catacombs.

"The nitre!" I said. "See, it increases. It hangs like moss upon the vaults. We are below the river's bed. The drops of moisture trickle among the bones. Come, we will go back before it is too late. Your cough—"

"It is nothing," he insisted. "Let us go on. But first, another drink of the Medoc."

I broke a bottle of de Grâve[12] and handed it to him. He emptied it at a breath. His eyes flashed with a fierce light. He laughed and threw the bottle upward with a motion I did not understand.

I looked at him in surprise. He repeated the movement—a **grotesque** one.

"You do not understand?" he said.

"Not I," I replied.

"Then you are not of the brotherhood."

"What do you mean?"

"You are not of the masons."[13]

"Oh yes, yes," I said. "Yes, yes."

"You? Impossible! A mason?"

"A mason," I replied.

"A sign," he said.

"It is this," I answered. I produced a trowel[14] from beneath the folds of my cloak.

"You jest!" he exclaimed, **recoiling** a few paces. "But let us go on to the Amontillado."

"Be it so," I said, replacing the tool beneath my cloak. I offered him my arm, and he leaned upon it heavily. We

[11]*Nemo me impune lacessit* means "No one insults me without punishment" in Latin.

[12]De Grâve is a Bordeaux wine.

[13]Fortunato is referring to the Freemasons, an international organization with secret rites and signs.

[14]A trowel is a hand tool with a flat blade.

continued on our way in search of the Amontillado. We passed through a range of low arches. We **descended,** walked a ways, and descended again, arriving at a deep crypt.[15] Here the foulness of the air caused our torches to glow rather than flame.

At the far end of the crypt was another smaller one. Its walls had been lined with human remains. They were piled up to the vault overhead in the style of the great catacombs of Paris. Three sides of this **interior** crypt were still decorated in this manner. From the fourth side, the bones had been thrown down. The bones lay scattered upon the earth, forming a mound of some size.

A wall was exposed by the removal of the bones. Inside it, we saw still another space. It was about four feet deep, three wide, and six or seven high. It seemed to have been built for no special use. It was merely the space between two of the huge supports of the roof. It was backed by a wall of solid granite.[16]

Fortunato lifted up his dull torch. But it was in vain that he tried to see into the depths of the recess. The **feeble** light did not let us see its end.

"Go on," I said. "In here is the Amontillado. As for Luchesi—"

"He is an **ignoramus,**" interrupted my friend. He stepped unsteadily forward. I followed right at his heels. He had reached the end of the space in an instant. Finding his progress stopped by the rock, he stood, stupidly confused.

A moment more, and I had chained him to the granite. In its surface were two iron staples. They were about two feet apart from one another. From one of these staples hung a short chain; from the other hung a padlock. I threw the links about his waist. It took but a few seconds to fasten it. He was much too shocked to resist. Withdrawing the key, I stepped back from the recess.

"Pass your hand over the wall," I said. "You cannot help feeling the nitre. Indeed it is *very* damp. Once more

[15]A crypt is an underground room that is used as a burial place.
[16]Granite is a hard rock used for building.

let me *beg* you to return. No? Then I shall certainly leave you. But I must first do what little I can to make you feel at home."

"The Amontillado!" cried my friend. He had not yet recovered from his shock.

"True," I replied. "The Amontillado."

As I said these words, I busied myself. I dug among the pile of bones. Throwing them aside, I soon uncovered a supply of building stone and mortar. I made use of these materials and my trowel. I began to **vigorously** wall up the entrance of the space.

I had hardly laid the first row of masonry when I discovered that Fortunato's intoxication had mostly worn off. The earliest sign was a low moaning cry from the depths of the recess. It was *not* the cry of a drunken man.

Then there was a long and stubborn silence. I laid the second row, and the third, and the fourth. Then I heard the furious shaking of the chain. The noise lasted for several minutes. To listen to it with more enjoyment, I stopped my work and sat down upon the bones.

When at last the clanking stopped, I took up my trowel again. I finished the fifth, the sixth, and the seventh rows without interruption. The wall was now nearly level with my chest. I again paused and held the torch over the mason-work. It threw a few feeble rays upon the figure within.

Suddenly, a series of loud and shrill screams burst from the throat of the chained form. They drove me back violently. For a brief moment, I hesitated—I trembled.

Unsheathing[17] my sword, I began to **grope** with it about the recess. But a moment's thought reassured me. I placed my hand upon the solid material of the catacombs and felt satisfied. I went back to the wall. I replied to the yells of him who cried out. I echoed—I aided—I surpassed them in volume and in strength. I did this, and the caller grew still.

---

[17] A sheath is a sword holder attached to a belt.

It was not yet midnight, and my task was drawing to a close. I had completed the eighth, the ninth, and the tenth levels. I had finished a part of the eleventh—the last. There remained but a single stone to be fitted and plastered in. I struggled with its weight. I put it partway in its intended place.

But now there came from out of the space a low laugh. It made the hairs on my head stand up. It was followed by a sad voice, one that I had difficulty recognizing as that of the noble Fortunato.

The voice said, "Ha! ha! ha!—hee! hee!—a very good joke indeed. An excellent jest. We will have many a rich laugh about it at the palazzo. Ho! ho! ho!—over our wine—ha! ha! ha!"

"The Amontillado!" I said.

"Hee! hee! hee!—hee! hee! hee!—yes, the Amontillado. But is it not getting late? Will not they be awaiting us at the palazzo, the Lady Fortunato and the rest? Let us be gone."

"Yes," I said, "let us be gone."

"For the love of God, Montresor!"

"Yes," I said, "for the love of God!"

But to these words I listened in vain for a reply. I grew impatient. I called aloud.

"Fortunato!"

No answer. I called again.

"Fortunato!"

No answer still. I thrust a torch through the remaining opening and let it fall within. Only a jingling of the bells came forth in reply. My heart grew sick—because of the dampness of the catacombs, of course.

I hurried to end my work. I forced the last stone into its position. I plastered it up. Against the new masonry, I replaced the old wall of bones. And for half of a century, no mortal has disturbed them.

In pace requiescat![18]

---

[18] *In pace requiescat* is Latin for "May he rest in peace."

INSIGHTS INTO
EDGAR ALLAN POE (1809–1849)

"**L**uchesi cannot tell Amontillado from Sherry," says Fortunato about a rival wine taster. But Amontillado really *is* a kind of sherry—and not even very fine sherry. So why all the fuss about Amontillado in Edgar Allan Poe's story? Why did Poe even choose this wine? He probably just liked the sound of the word.

This says a great deal about how Poe wrote. He was very concerned with how his stories and poems affected the reader. He was particularly concerned with the sounds of words. Many of his poems seem more like music than poetry.

Poe became an orphan early in life. His middle name, Allan, was the last name of his childhood guardian. As a youth, Poe attended several schools, but he always left for one reason or another. He was expelled from West Point.

When Poe was twenty-seven, he married his thirteen-year-old cousin, Virginia Clem. For a decade after that, he lived with Virginia and her mother, Maria. Then Virginia died. After that, Maria was Poe's only source of support and encouragement.

Poe was in desperate need of support and encouragement. He was an extremely hardworking editor, writer, and critic. Even so, he was usually very poor. But during his life, he did become famous for writing his poem "The Raven."

Many of his poems are about grief and despair. His most famous stories, like "The Cask of Amontillado," deal with horrifying situations. But Poe wrote in a wide variety of styles. He also wrote humorous stories and is credited with inventing the modern detective mystery.

Poe died mysteriously in Baltimore, Maryland. He was very drunk at the time of his death. It was election day, and perhaps he fell victim to "repeaters." These were

38

people who got strangers drunk to persuade them to vote a certain way—sometimes more than once. It was a strange end to a strange, sad life.

Other works by Edgar Allan Poe:
"The Bells," poem
"Annabel Lee," poem
"The Fall of the House of Usher," short story
"The Raven," poem
"The Tell-Tale Heart," short story

THE BRAZILIAN CAT

SIR ARTHUR CONAN DOYLE

VOCABULARY PREVIEW

Below is a list of words that appear in the story. Read the list and get to know the words before you start the story.

aggressive—forceful; on the attack
breach—violation
carnivore—flesh-eating mammal
coincidence—chance happening
compliment—praise; flattery
diabolical—evil
eavesdropper—one who listens in on others' conversations
hospitable—welcoming; friendly; generous
inheritance—money or property received upon someone's death
leverage—force or weight
occasional—rare; infrequent
occupants—residents
offensive—rude; insulting
poverty—neediness; poorness
privileged—favored; given special rights
profession—job; career
sinister—mean; devilish
treacherous—deceiving; double-crossing; disloyal
vague—unclear; weak
vulnerable—unprotected; open to attack

THE

BRAZILIAN

CAT

Which is more dangerous, a wild animal or a greedy human? When money is involved, a person can become very treacherous and bloodthirsty. Especially when a dangerous animal is involved.

It can be hard for a young fellow to have expensive tastes, great expectations, and aristocratic[1] relatives. It is hard luck indeed if he has those—but no actual money in his pocket. And it is worse if he has no **profession** by which he may earn his own money.

My father was a good, cheerful, easygoing man. The fact was that he trusted in the wealth and generosity of his unmarried elder brother, Lord Southerton. My father took it for granted that I would never be called upon to earn a living for myself.

[1]An aristocrat is a member of a ruling class or the nobility.

I was his only son. He imagined that there would be a place for me on the great Southerton Estates.[2] Or if not that, then at least there would be found for me some position in the diplomatic service.[3] That still remains the special shelter of our **privileged** classes.

My father died too early to realize how false his hopes had been. Neither my uncle nor the nation took the slightest notice of me. They showed no interest in my career. An **occasional** pair of pheasants or basket of hares was all that anyone gave me. It was all that reminded me that I was heir[4] to Otwell House, one of the richest estates in the country.

In the meantime, I found myself unmarried and a man-about-town. I lived in a group of apartments in Grosvenor Mansions.[5] But I had no work except that of pigeon-shooting and polo-playing.

Month by month, I realized that it was increasingly difficult to put off bill collectors. And it became harder and harder to borrow money when I owed so much. Ruin lay right across my path. Every day I saw it clearer, nearer, and more absolutely unavoidable.

Apart from the great wealth of Lord Southerton, all of my other relatives were fairly well-to-do. That made me feel my own **poverty** all the more. The closest of these was Everard King, my father's nephew and my own first cousin. He had spent an adventurous life in Brazil. Now he had returned to this country to settle down with his fortune.

We never knew how he made his money, but he seemed to have plenty of it. He bought the estate of Greylands, near Clipton-on-the-Marsh, in Suffolk.[6]

For the first year he lived in England, he took no more notice of me than my stingy uncle did. But at last one summer morning, I received a letter asking me to come down that very day. I was invited to spend a short visit at Greylands Court.

[2]An estate is a large mansion and its surrounding land.
[3]A position in diplomatic service means being an ambassador to a foreign country.
[4]An heir is a person who receives the property of a relative who has died.
[5]Grosvenor Square is in central London.
[6]Suffolk is in eastern England.

I was greatly relieved. I was expecting a rather long visit to Bankruptcy Court[7] at the time. This break seemed miraculous.

I thought that if I could only get on good terms with this unknown relative of mine, I might pull through yet. For the sake of the family, he could not let me go entirely to the wall. I ordered my valet[8] to pack my suitcase. And I set off the same evening for Clipton-on-the-Marsh.

After changing at Ipswich,[9] a little local train left me at a small, deserted station. The station lay in a rolling, grassy countryside. A sluggish and winding river curved in and out among the valleys. The high, sandy banks showed that we were within reach of the tide.

No carriage was waiting for me. (I found out afterward that my telegram had been delayed.) So I hired a one-horse cart at the local inn. The driver, an excellent fellow, was full of my relative's praises. I learned from him that Mr. Everard King was a magic name in that part of the country.

My cousin had entertained the schoolchildren. He had thrown his grounds open to visitors. He had supported charities. In short, his kindness had been so complete that my driver could only explain it in one way—he thought that Mr. Everard King had parliamentary[10] ambitions.

My attention was drawn away from my driver's praise. A very beautiful bird had appeared and settled on a telegraph pole beside the road. At first, I thought it was a jay, but it was larger, with brighter feathers. The driver explained its presence at once. He said that it belonged to the very man we were about to visit.

It seems that getting foreign creatures to live in our climate was one of my cousin's hobbies. He had brought with him from Brazil a number of birds and beasts. He was trying to raise them in England.

[7]A bankruptcy court settles the financial difficulties of people who cannot pay their debts.
[8]A valet is a man's male servant.
[9]Ipswich is a town in eastern England near the North Sea.
[10]Parliament is the national legislature of England.

When once we had passed the gates of Greylands Park, we saw plenty of signs of this taste of his. I saw some small spotted deer and a curious wild pig known as a peccary. There was a gorgeously feathered oriole and some sort of armadillo. And an unusual, clumsy beast with turned-in toes that looked like a very fat badger.

Mr. Everard King, my unknown cousin, was standing upon the steps of his house. He had seen us in the distance and guessed that it was I.

He looked very plain and kind. He was short and stout, forty-five years old, perhaps. His round, good-humored face was burned brown with the tropical sun and shot with a thousand wrinkles.

He wore white linen clothes, in true planter style. He had a cigar between his lips and a large Panama hat[11] upon the back of his head.

It was such a figure as one thinks of in front of a bungalow[12] with a porch. He looked curiously out of place in front of this broad English mansion. It had solid wings and Palladio[13] pillars in front of the doorway.

"My dear!" he cried, glancing over his shoulder. "My dear, here is our guest! Welcome, welcome to Greylands! I am delighted to meet you, Cousin Marshall. I take it as a great **compliment** that you should honor this sleepy little country place with your presence."

Nothing could have been more warm and friendly than his manner. He set me at my ease in an instant. But all of his friendliness was needed to make up for the coldness and even rudeness of his wife.

She was a tall, worried-looking woman who came at his call. She was, I believe, of Brazilian background, though she spoke excellent English. I excused her manners because of her ignorance of our customs.

She did not attempt to hide her feelings, however, either then or afterward. She made it clear that I was not a very welcome visitor at Greylands Court.

[11]A Panama hat is made from leaves of the jipijapa plant of South and Central America.
[12]A bungalow is a simple one-story house with a broad porch.
[13]Palladio was an Italian architect who developed a style based on the classic buildings of ancient Rome.

Her actual words were polite. But she had very expressive, dark eyes, and I read in them very clearly from the first that she strongly wished me back in London.

However, my debts were pressing. My plans for my wealthy relative were important. I could not allow them to be upset by the ill temper of his wife. So I ignored her coldness and returned the warmth of his welcome.

No pains had been spared by him to make me comfortable. My room was a charming one. He begged me to tell him anything that could add to my happiness.

It was on the tip of my tongue to inform him that a blank check would be of great help toward that end. But I felt that it might be too soon in the present state of our friendship.

The dinner was excellent. We sat together afterward over his cigars and coffee. Later, he told me the coffee was specially prepared upon his own plantation.[14] It seemed to me that all of my driver's praises were justified. I thought that I had never met a more large-hearted and **hospitable** man.

Despite his cheery good nature, he was a man with a strong will. He had a fiery temper of his own. Of this I had an example upon the following morning.

The curious dislike that Mrs. Everard King had formed toward me was strong. Her manner at breakfast was almost **offensive.** But her meaning became unmistakable when her husband left the room.

"The best train in the day is a twelve-fifteen," she said.

"But I was not thinking of going today," I answered honestly—perhaps even boldly. I was determined not to be driven out by this woman.

"Oh—if it rests with you—" said she. Then she stopped with a shameless expression in her eyes.

"I am sure," I answered, "that Mr. Everard King would tell me if I were outstaying my welcome."

[14]A plantation is a large farming estate.

"What's this? What's this?" said a voice. And there he was in the room. He had overheard my last words. A glance at our faces had told him the rest. In an instant, his chubby, cheery face set into an expression of utter fierceness.

"Might I trouble you to walk outside, Marshall?" he asked. (I may mention that my own name is Marshall King.)

He closed the door behind me. Then, for an instant, I heard him talking in a low voice of strong feeling to his wife. This terrible **breach** of hospitality seemed to have hit upon his most sensitive point. I am no **eavesdropper,** so I walked out onto the lawn.

Soon I heard a hurried step behind me. There was the lady. Her face was pale with excitement and her eyes red with tears.

"My husband has asked me to apologize to you, Mr. Marshall King," she said. She stood with downcast eyes before me.

"Please do not say another word, Mrs. King."

Her dark eyes suddenly blazed out at me.

"You fool!" she hissed with frantic anger. Turning on her heel, she swept back to the house.

The insult was shocking and hateful. I could only stand staring after her in confusion. I was still there when my host joined me. He was his cheerful self again.

"I hope that my wife has apologized for her foolish remarks," he said.

"Oh, yes—yes, certainly!"

He put his hand through my arm and walked with me up and down the lawn.

"You must not take it seriously," he said. "It would make me terribly unhappy if you cut short your visit by one hour. There is no reason why there should be anything hidden between relatives. The fact is that my poor dear wife is terribly jealous. She hates that anyone—male or female—should for an instant come between us.

"Her ideal is a desert island and a never-ending *tête-à-tête*.[15] That gives you a clue to her actions. They are, I confess, on this particular point, not far removed from madness. Tell me that you will think no more of it."

"No, no. Certainly not."

"Then light this cigar. Come 'round with me and see my little menagerie."[16]

The whole afternoon was taken up by this tour. It included all the birds, beasts, and even reptiles that he had imported. He spoke eagerly of his successes and his failures, his births and his deaths.

As we walked, some colorful bird would flutter up from the grass. Or some curious beast would slink into cover. Each time, Everard King would cry out in delight like a schoolboy.

Finally, he led me down a hallway that extended from one wing of the house. At the end of this was a heavy door. The door had an opening in it with a sliding shutter. Beside the door, an iron handle stuck out from the wall. The handle was attached to a wheel. A line of strong bars extended across the hall.

"I am about to show you the jewel of my collection," said Everard. "There is only one other in Europe. It is a Brazilian cat."

"But how does that differ from any other cat?"

"You will soon see that," he said, laughing. "Will you kindly open that shutter and look through?"

I did so, and I found that I was gazing into a large, empty room. It had a stone floor and small barred windows upon the farther wall. In the center of this room was a huge creature. It was stretched out in the middle of a golden patch of sunlight. It was as large as a tiger, but as black and sleek as ebony.[17]

It was simply a very huge and very well-kept cat. It cuddled up and sunned itself in that yellow pool of light

---

[15]*Tête-à-tête*, French for "head-to-head," means a private conversation between two people.

[16]A menagerie is a collection of live wild animals, as in a zoo.

[17]Ebony is hard, dark-colored wood.

exactly as a cat would do. It was graceful, powerful, and smoothly **diabolical.** I could not take my eyes from the opening.

"Isn't he splendid?" said my host excitedly.

"Glorious! I never saw such a noble creature."

"Some people call it a black puma,[18] but really it is not a puma at all. That fellow is nearly eleven feet from tail to tip. Four years ago, he was a little ball of black fluff, with two yellow eyes staring out of it. He was sold to me as a newborn cub up in the wild country at the headwaters of the Rio Negro.[19] They speared his mother to death after she had killed a dozen of them."

"They are fierce, then?"

"The most absolutely **treacherous** and bloodthirsty creatures upon earth. You talk about a Brazilian cat to a forest native and see him get the jumps. They prefer humans to game.

"This fellow has not yet tasted living blood. But when he does, he will be a terror. At present, he won't stand anyone but me in his den. Even Baldwin, the groom, dares not go near him. As to me, I am his mother and father in one."

As he spoke, to my surprise, he opened the door and slipped in. He closed the door instantly behind him. At the sound of his voice, the huge, graceful creature rose and yawned. It rubbed its black head happily against Everard's side.

"Now, Tommy, into your cage!" he said fondly.

The huge cat walked over to one side of the room and coiled up under a framework of bars. Everard King came out. Taking the iron handle I mentioned, he began to turn it. As he did so, the line of bars in the hallway began to move. They passed through a slot in the wall and closed up the front of the barred area. It made a good cage.

When it was in position, he opened the door again and invited me into the room. The air was heavy with the strong, musty smell of the great **carnivore.**

[18]A puma is a mountain lion, a large, powerful, wild cat.
[19]The Rio Negro is a river in southern Brazil.

"That's how we work it," he said. "We give him the run of the room for exercise. Then at night we put him in his cage. You can let him out by turning the handle from the passage. Or, as you have seen, you can coop him up in the same way. No, no, you should not do that!"

I had put my hand between the bars to pat the glossy, heaving flank. He pulled it back, with a serious face.

"I promise you that he is not safe. Don't imagine that because I can take liberties with him anyone else can. The cat is very choosy in his friends—aren't you, Tommy? Ah, he hears his lunch coming to him! Don't you, boy?"

A step sounded in the stone-floored passage. The creature had sprung to his feet and was pacing up and down the narrow cage. His yellow eyes were gleaming. His red tongue was rippling and licking over the white line of his jagged teeth.

A groom entered with a rough joint of meat upon a tray and thrust it through the bars to him. The cat pounced lightly upon it and carried it off to the corner. There the creature held it between his paws, tearing and twisting at it. The cat raised his bloody muzzle every now and then to look at us. It was an evil, yet enormously interesting, sight.

"You can't wonder that I am fond of him, can you?" said my host, as we left the room. "Especially when you think that I have raised him. It was no joke bringing him over from the center of South America. But here he is. Safe and sound.

"As I have said," my cousin went on, "he is by far the most perfect Brazilian cat in Europe. The people at the zoo are dying to have him, but I really can't part with him. Now then, I think that perhaps I have pushed my hobby upon you long enough. We cannot do better than follow Tommy's example and go to our lunch."

My South American relative was deeply involved with his grounds and their curious **occupants.** I hardly gave him credit at first for having any interests outside them. But apparently he did have some, and they were important ones. That was shown by the number of telegrams he received. They arrived at all hours. They were always opened by him with great eagerness.

Sometimes I imagined that it must be the Turf,[20] and sometimes the Stock Exchange. But he certainly had some very urgent business going on. And it was not carried out upon the hills of Suffolk. During the six days of my visit, he had no fewer than three or four telegrams a day—sometimes as many as seven or eight.

I had filled these six days well. By the end of them, I had succeeded in getting on the most friendly terms with my cousin. We sat up late in the billiard room every night. He told me the most wonderful stories of his adventures in America—desperate and reckless stories. I could hardly connect them with the man before me.

In return, I offered some of my own memories of London life. They interested him very much. So much so, that he vowed he would come up to Grosvenor Mansions and stay with me. He was eager to see the faster side of city life. Certainly, even though I say it, he could not have chosen a better guide.

It was not until the last day of my visit that I dared bring up what was on my mind. I told him honestly about my financial problems and my oncoming ruin. He listened carefully, puffing hard at his cigar.

"But surely," he said, "you are the heir of our relative, Lord Southerton."

"I have every reason to believe so. But he would never give me any allowance."

"No, no, of course not. I have heard of his stingy ways. My poor Marshall, your position has been a very hard one. By the way, have you heard any news of Lord Southerton's health lately?"

"He has always been in a serious condition ever since my childhood."

"Exactly—a creaking hinge, if ever there was one. Your **inheritance** may be a long way off. Dear me, what a difficult fix you are in!"

---

[20]The Turf refers to horse racing.

"I had some hopes, sir, that when you knew all the facts—that you might be willing to advance—"

"Don't say another word, my dear boy!" he cried with the greatest warmth. "We shall talk it over tonight. I give you my word that whatever is in my power shall be done."

I was not sorry that my visit was drawing to a close. It is unpleasant to feel that there is one person in the house who eagerly desires your departure.

Mrs. King's pale face and forbidding eyes had become increasingly hateful to me. She was no longer actually rude. Her fear of her husband prevented that. But she pushed her insane jealousy so far as to ignore me.

She never spoke to me. In every way, she made my stay at Greylands as uncomfortable as she could. Her manner was worse during that last day. I would certainly have left had it not been for that meeting with my host in the evening. That would, I hoped, repair my broken fortunes.

It was very late when it took place. My relative had received even more telegrams than usual that day. He went off to his study after dinner. He came out only when the servants had gone to bed.

I heard him go around locking the doors, as was his habit at night. Finally, he joined me in the billiard room. His stout figure was wrapped in a dressing gown. He wore a pair of red Turkish slippers without any heels.

Settling into an armchair, he made himself a glass of grog.[21] I could not help noticing that he used much more whisky than water.

"My word!" he exclaimed. "What a night!"

It was, indeed. The wind was howling and screaming around the house. The shuttered windows rattled and shook as if they were coming in. It made the glow of the yellow lamps seem brighter. And the taste of our cigars was also sweeter because of the contrast.

"Now, my boy," said my host, "we have the house and the night to ourselves. Let me have an idea of how your

[21]Grog is an alcoholic drink.

finances stand. I will see what can be done to set them in order. I wish to hear every detail."

Thus encouraged, I started to explain everything. Everybody I did business with and owed money to figured into the story—from my landlord to my valet.

I had notes in my pocketbook. I brought forth my facts and gave, I flatter myself, a very businesslike statement. I told him all about my own unbusinesslike ways and miserable position.

I was unhappy, however, to notice that my companion's eyes were empty. His mind was somewhere else. When he did sometimes make a remark, it was with little interest and was completely pointless. I was sure he had not followed my remarks at all.

He roused himself every now and then to put on some show of interest. He asked me to repeat or to explain more fully. But then he always sank again into the same dark gloom. At last, he rose and threw the end of his cigar into the fire.

"I'll tell you what, my boy," he said. "I never had a head for figures, so excuse me. You must jot it all down upon paper. Let me have a note of the amount. I'll understand it when I see it in black and white."

The request was encouraging, and I promised to do so.

"And now it's time we were in bed. By Jove, there's one o'clock striking in the hall."

The tingling of the chiming clock broke through the deep roar of the storm. The wind was sweeping past with the rush of a great river.

"I must see my cat before I go to bed," said my host. "A high wind excites him. Will you come?"

"Certainly," I said.

"Then step softly—and don't speak. Everyone is asleep."

We passed quietly down the lamp-lit hall. We went through the door at the farther end. All was dark in the stone hallway, but a stable lantern hung on a hook. My host took it down and lit it. There were no bars visible in the hall, so I knew that the beast was in its cage.

"Come in!" said my relative.

We heard a deep growling as we entered. The storm had really excited the creature. We could see it in the flickering light of the lantern. The huge black mass was coiled in the corner of its den. Its tail switched angrily in the straw. The light threw a squat, rough shadow upon the whitewashed[22] wall.

"Poor Tommy is not in the best of temper," said Everard King. He held up the lantern and looked in at the cat. "What a black devil he looks, doesn't he? I must give him a little supper to put him in a better mood. Would you mind holding the lantern for a moment?"

I took it from his hand, and he stepped to the door.

"His store of food is just outside here," he said. "You will excuse me for an instant, won't you?" He went out. The door shut with a sharp metallic click behind him.

That hard, crisp sound made my heart stand still. A sudden wave of terror passed over me. A **vague** understanding of some horrible treachery turned me cold. I sprang to the door, but there was no handle on the inside.

"Here!" I cried. "Let me out!"

"All right! Don't make a fuss!" said my host from the hallway. "You've got the light all right."

"Yes, but I don't care for being locked in alone like this."

"Don't you?" I heard his warm, chuckling laugh. "You won't be alone long."

"Let me out, sir!" I demanded angrily. "I tell you, I don't allow practical jokes of this sort."

"Practical is the word," he chuckled hatefully. And then suddenly, I heard something else over the roar of the storm. I heard the creak and whine of the handle turning. I heard the rattle of the bars as they passed through the slot. Great God! He was letting loose the Brazilian cat!

---

[22]Whitewash is a mixture of lime and water used to whiten walls and fences.

In the light of the lantern, I saw the bars sliding slowly in front of me. Already there was an opening a foot wide at the farther end. With a scream, I seized the last bar with my hands. I pulled with the strength of a madman. I *was* a madman with rage and horror.

For a minute or more, I held the thing motionless. I knew that he was straining with all of his force upon the handle. I knew the **leverage** was sure to overcome me. I gave way inch by inch, my feet sliding along the stones. All the time I begged and prayed for this inhuman monster to save me from this horrible death.

I tried to use his kinship. I reminded him that I was his guest. I begged to know what harm I had ever done him. His only answers were the tugs and jerks on the handle. Each tug, despite all of my struggles, pulled another bar through the opening.

Clinging and clutching, I was dragged across the whole front of the cage. My wrists ached, and my fingers were scraped. I gave up the hopeless struggle.

The bars clanged back as I released them. An instant later, I heard the shuffle of the Turkish slippers in the hall. And I heard the slam of the distant door. Then everything was silent.

The creature had not moved during this time. He lay still in the corner. His tail had stopped switching. Clinging to his bars, I had been dragged screaming across in front of him. This vision seemed to have filled him with surprise. I saw his great eyes staring steadily at me.

I had dropped the lantern when I grabbed the bars, but it still burned on the floor. I made a move to get it. I had some idea that its light might protect me. But the instant I moved, the beast gave a deep and threatening growl. I stopped and stood still, shaking with fear in every limb.

The cat (if one may call such a dreadful creature by such a plain name) was not more than ten feet from me. The eyes were shining like miniature balls of phosphorus[23] in the darkness. They horrified and fascinated me all at once. I could not take my own eyes from them.

[23]Phosphorus is a natural element that glows.

Nature plays strange tricks on us at such tense moments. Those glowing lights grew stronger and weaker with a steady rhythm. Sometimes they seemed to be tiny points of great brightness. They were like little electric sparks in the black darkness. Then they would widen and widen. Soon, all that corner of the room was filled with their shifting, **sinister** light. And then they went out completely.

The beast had closed its eyes. I do not know whether there is any truth to the old idea that humans can control animals by their gaze. Perhaps the huge cat was simply drowsy. But the fact remains that it showed no sign of attacking me. It simply rested its sleek, black head upon its huge forepaws and seemed to sleep.

I stood still, fearing to move lest I rouse it into dangerous life once more. But at least I was able to think clearly now.

Here I was, shut up for the night with the fierce beast. My instincts warned me that the animal was as savage as its master. I had also been warned by the believable villain who laid this trap for me. How could I hold it off until morning?

The door was hopeless. So were the narrow, barred windows. There was no hope anywhere in the stone-floored room. To cry for help was absurd. I knew that this den was too far from the rest of the house. The hallway that connected with the house was at least a hundred feet long.

Besides, the storm was thundering outside. My cries were not likely to be heard. I had only my own courage and my own wits to trust.

And then, my eyes fell upon the lantern. I felt a fresh wave of horror. The candle had burned low and was already beginning to sputter. Soon it would be out.

I had only ten minutes, then, in which to do something. After that, I would be left in the dark with that fearful beast. I felt that I would be unable to act.

The very thought of it froze me in place. I cast my hopeless eyes around this chamber of death. They rested upon one spot that seemed to promise—not safety—but it offered less firsthand and direct danger than the open floor.

I have said that the cage had a top as well as a front. This top framework was left standing when the front was wound through the slot in the wall. It consisted of bars a few inches apart, with strong wire netting in between. It stood now as a great barred roof over the crouching figure in the corner. The space between this iron shelf and the roof may have been about two or three feet.

If only I could get up there. Squeezed between the bars and ceiling, I would have only one **vulnerable** side. I would be safe from below, from behind, and from each side. I could only be attacked on the open side of it. It is true that I had no protection whatever. But at least I would be out of the brute's path when he began to pace around his den. He would have to come out of his way to reach me.

It was now or never. Once the light was out, it would be impossible. With a gulp in my throat, I sprang up. I seized the iron edge of the top framework and swung myself panting onto it. I wiggled in, face downward. I found myself looking straight into the terrible eyes and yawning jaws of the cat. Its stinking breath came up into my face like the steam from some foul pot.

It appeared, however, to be curious rather than angry. With a sleek ripple of its long black back, it rose. It stretched itself and reared on its hind legs with one forepaw against the wall. It raised the other paw and drew its claws across the wire mesh beneath me. I should mention, I was still in evening dress. One sharp white hook tore through my trousers and dug a gouge in my knee.

It was not meant as an attack, but rather as an experiment. When I gave a sharp cry of pain, he dropped down again. Springing lightly into the room, he began walking swiftly around it. He looked up in my direction every now and again.

For my part, I shuffled backward until I lay with my back against the wall. I tucked myself into the smallest space possible. The farther I got, the more difficult it was for him to attack me.

He seemed more excited now that he had begun to move about. He ran swiftly and noiselessly around the den. He kept passing underneath the iron couch upon which I lay. It was awesome to see such a great thing passing like a shadow. His velvety pads made barely the softest thudding.

The candle was burning low—so low that I could hardly see the creature. And then, with a last spark and a sputter, it went out completely. I was alone with the cat in the dark!

When faced with danger, it helps to know that one has done all that can possibly be done. There is nothing to do then but quietly await the result. In this case, there was no chance for safety anywhere except in the exact spot where I was.

I stretched myself out and lay silently, almost breathlessly. I hoped that the beast might forget my presence. I reckoned that it must be two o'clock already. At four o'clock, it would be full dawn. I had no more than two hours to wait for daylight.

Outside, the storm still raged. The rain lashed continually against the little windows. Inside, the poisonous, stinking air was overpowering. I could neither hear nor see the cat.

I tried to think about other things. But only one thought had power enough to draw my mind from my terrible position—the thought of my cousin's wickedness. I considered his unequaled betrayal and his terrible hatred of me. Beneath that friendly face lurked the spirit of a medieval assassin.[24]

As I thought of it, I saw more clearly how cleverly the thing had been arranged. He had apparently gone to bed

[24]These assassins believed it was their religious duty to murder enemies.

with the others. No doubt he had his witness to prove it. Then, unknown to them, he had slipped down. He had lured me into his den and left me.

His story would be so simple. He had left me to finish my cigar in the billiard room. I had gone down on my own to have a last look at the cat. I had entered the room without observing that the cage was open. And I had been caught. How could such a crime be blamed on him? Suspicion, perhaps—but proof, never!

How slowly those dreadful two hours went by! Once I heard a low, rasping sound I thought must be the creature licking its own fur. Several times those greenish eyes gleamed at me through the darkness. But it was never a fixed stare. My hopes grew stronger that my presence had either been forgotten or ignored.

At last, the least faint glimmer of light came through the windows. I first saw them dimly as two gray squares upon the black wall. Then gray turned to white, and I could see my terrible companion again. And, alas, he could see me!

It was clear to me that he was now in a much more dangerous mood. He was definitely more **aggressive** than when I had seen him last. The cold of the morning had annoyed him, and he was hungry as well.

With a constant growl, he paced swiftly up and down the far side of the room, away from my place of safety. His whiskers bristled angrily, and his tail switched and lashed. As he turned at the corners, his savage eyes looked up at me with a dreadful threat. I knew then that he meant to kill me.

Yet I found myself admiring the slinky grace of the devilish thing. Its rippling movements were long and curving. Its beautiful sides were glossy. Its red tongue, which hung from the jet-black muzzle, was bright and throbbing. And all that time, its threatening growl was rising and rising to a peak. I knew that the crisis was at hand.

It was a miserable hour to meet such a death—so cold, so comfortless. I was shivering in my light dress clothes on this framework of torment. I tried to brace myself for it, to raise my soul above it.

At the same time, I felt the clear-headedness that comes to a perfectly desperate man. I looked around for some possible means of escape. One thing was clear to me. I knew that if the front of the cage were back in its place, I could find sure safety behind it. Could I possibly pull it back?

I hardly dared to move for fear of bringing the creature upon me. Slowly, very slowly, I put my hand forward. I grasped the edge of the front, the final bar that stuck through the wall. To my surprise, it came easily when I jerked it.

Of course, the difficulty of pulling it out arose from the fact that I was clinging to it. I pulled again, and three inches of it came through. It apparently ran on wheels. I pulled again . . . and then the cat sprang!

It was so quick, so sudden, that I never saw it happen. I simply heard the savage snarl. In another instant, I saw the blazing yellow eyes. The flattened black head, with its red tongue and flashing teeth, was within reach of me.

The impact of the creature shook the bars upon which I lay. I thought that the bars were coming down.

The cat swayed there for a moment. Its head and front paws were quite close to me. The hind paws clawed to find a grip upon the edge of the grating. I heard the claws rasping as they clung to the wire netting. The breath of the beast made me ill.

But its bound had been misjudged. It could not keep its position. It scratched madly at the bars. Slowly, grinning with rage, it swung backward. It dropped heavily onto the floor. With a growl, it turned to face me. It crouched for another spring.

I knew that the next few moments would decide what became of me. The creature had learned by experience. It would not misjudge again. If I was to have a chance for life, I knew that I had to act quickly and fearlessly. So I quickly formed my plan.

Pulling off my coat, I threw it down over the head of the beast. At the same moment, I dropped over the edge. I seized the end of the front grating and frantically pulled it out of the wall.

It came more easily than I could have expected. I rushed across the room, pulling it with me. But in my haste, I accidentally ended up on the outer side of the grate. Had it been the other way, I might have come off unmarked.

As it was, there was a moment's pause as I tried to pass through the opening I had left before. That pause was enough for the creature to toss off the coat and spring toward me.

I hurled myself through the gap and pulled the rails shut behind me. But he seized my leg before I could completely withdraw it. One stroke of that huge paw tore off my calf like a plane shaving wood curls.

The next moment, bleeding and fainting, I was lying in the foul straw inside the creature's den. A line of friendly bars was between the cat and me. He threw himself frantically against them.

I was too wounded to move and too faint to be aware of fear. I could only lie, more dead than alive, and watch the creature. It pressed its broad, black chest against the bars. It angled for me with its crooked paws. (I have seen a kitten do that with a trapped mouse.)

The cat ripped at my clothes. But, stretch as it would, it could not reach me. I had heard of the strange numbing effect produced by wounds from great carnivores. Now I was destined to experience it.

I had lost all sense of personality. I had little interest in the cat's failure or success. It was like watching some great game.

Gradually, my mind drifted into strange, hazy dreams. That black face and red tongue were in them all. And so I lost myself in the heaven of delirium.[25] That is the blessed relief of those who are too sorely tried.

Afterward, I traced the course of events. I realized that I must have been unconscious for about two hours. What roused me to consciousness again was that sharp metallic click. It had been the beginning of my terrible experience. It was the shooting back of the spring lock.

My senses were not clear enough to completely understand what they saw. I became aware of the round, kind face of my cousin peering through the open door. What he saw seemed to amaze him.

There was the cat crouching on the floor. I was stretched upon my back within the cage. I was in my shirt-sleeves, and my trousers were torn to ribbons. A pool of blood was all around me.

I can still see his amazed face with the morning sunlight upon it. He peered at me and peered again. He closed the door behind him and came over to the cage to see if I were really dead. Then he turned to look at the animal.

"Good old Tommy!" he cried. "Good old Tommy!"

Then he came near the bars, his back still toward me.

"Down, you stupid beast!" he roared. "Down, sir! Don't you know your master?"

Suddenly, even in my muddled brain, the memory of his words came to me. He had said that the taste of blood would turn the cat into a monster. My blood had done it, but he would pay the price.

"Get away!" he screamed. "Get away, you devil! Baldwin! Baldwin! Oh, my God!"

I heard him fall, and rise, and fall again. There was a sound like the ripping of heavy cloth. His screams grew fainter until they were lost in the teasing snarl.

And then, after I thought that he was dead, I saw him again. As if in a nightmare, a blinded, tattered, blood-soaked figure ran wildly around the room. And that was the last glimpse I had of him before I fainted again.

[25]Delirium is temporary mental confusion.

I was many months in my recovery. In fact, I cannot say that I ever recovered fully. To the end of my days, I shall carry a cane as a sign of my night with the Brazilian cat.

Baldwin, the groom, and the other servants could not tell what had happened. Drawn by the cries of their master, they found me behind the bars. His remains—or what they later discovered to be his remains—were in the clutch of the creature he had reared.

They drove the cat off with hot irons and shot it through the slot in the door. Finally, they got me out of there. I was carried to my bedroom, where I rested under the roof of my would-be murderer.

I remained between life and death for several weeks. They had sent for a surgeon from Clipton and a nurse from London. In a month, I was able to be carried to the station. Then I was taken back to Grosvenor Mansions.

I have one memory of that time. If it was not so clearly fixed in my memory, I might think it was one of many visions made up by a delirious brain.

One night, when the nurse was absent, the door to my room opened. A tall woman in blackest mourning clothes slipped into the room. She came across to me.

As she bent her pale face, I saw her by the faint gleam of the night-light. It was the Brazilian woman—my cousin's widow. She stared hard into my face. Her expression was kinder than I had ever seen it.

"Are you conscious?" she asked.

I nodded feebly, for I was still very weak.

"Well then," she began, "I only wished to say to you that you have yourself to blame. Did I not do all I could for you? From the beginning, I tried to drive you from the house. By every means, short of betraying my husband, I tried to save you from him. I knew that he had a reason for bringing you here. I knew that he would never let you get away."

Looking toward the door, she paused. Her dark eyes were full of pain as she continued. "No one knew him as I knew him. I suffered from him so often. I did not dare to tell you all this. He would have killed me. But I did my best for you."

Her voice faltered, but she went on. "As things have turned out, you have been the best friend that I have ever had. You have set me free. I believed that nothing but death would do that. I am sorry if you are hurt, but I cannot blame myself. I told you that you were a fool—and a fool you have been."

She crept out of the room, the bitter, strange woman. I was never to see her again. With what remained of her husband's property, she went back to her native land. I have heard that she took the veil there.[26]

It was not until I had been back in London for some time that the doctors said I was well enough to do business. It was not a very welcome permission for me. I feared that it would be the signal for a rush of people to whom I owed money. But it was Summers, my lawyer, who first came to see me.

"I am very glad to see that your lordship is so much better," said he. "I have been waiting for a long time to offer my congratulations."

"What do you mean, Summers? This is no time for joking."

"I mean what I say," he answered. "You have been Lord Southerton for the last six weeks. We feared that it would slow your recovery if you were to learn it sooner."

Lord Southerton! One of the richest nobles in England! I could not believe my ears. And then, suddenly, I thought of the time that had passed. It matched the time of my injuries.

"Then Lord Southerton must have died about the same time that I was hurt?"

"His death took place upon that very day." Summers looked hard at me as I spoke. I am convinced—for he was a very shrewd fellow—that he had guessed the true state of the case. He paused for a moment as if awaiting a secret from me. But I could not see what was to be gained by exposing such a family scandal.

[26]To take the veil is to become a nun.

"Yes, a very curious **coincidence,**" he continued, with the same knowing look. "Naturally, you are aware that your cousin Everard King was the next heir to the estates. Now, what if it had been you instead of him who had been torn to pieces by this tiger, or whatever it was? Then, of course, he would have been Lord Southerton right now."

"No doubt," said I.

"And he took such an interest in it," said Summers. "I happen to know that the late Lord Southerton's valet was in Mr. King's pay. Your cousin used to get telegrams from the valet every few hours. They told him how Lord Southerton was getting on.

"That would be about the time when you were down there. Was it not strange that your cousin should wish to be so well informed? He knew that he was not the direct heir."

"Very strange, indeed," I agreed. "And now, Summers, if you will, bring me my bills and a new checkbook. We will begin to get things into order."

INSIGHTS INTO SIR ARTHUR CONAN DOYLE   (1859–1930)

Arthur Conan Doyle did not start off as a writer but as a medical doctor. His practice was not very successful, so he started writing stories to make extra money. Before long, he was the highest-paid writer of his time, and he gave up his medical practice altogether.

Why were Doyle's stories an immediate success? Perhaps it was because in them, Doyle created the detective hero Sherlock Holmes. The public was wildly enthusiastic about Holmes stories.

Unfortunately, Doyle himself was not very fond of Holmes. He thought that such stories kept him away from more serious writing. To get rid of Holmes, Doyle wrote one story in which the detective seemingly died. The public outcry of disappointment was so great that Doyle had to bring Holmes back to life again.

If you have read "The Cask of Amontillado" in this volume, you may see some resemblance between Edgar Allan Poe's story and "The Brazilian Cat." This is because Doyle was deeply influenced by Poe. Even the character of Sherlock Holmes can be traced to the influence of Poe. It was Poe who pioneered the detective story.

Doyle created another hero named Professor Challenger, an adventurous scientist in *The Lost World.* This novel takes Challenger to a mysterious place where dinosaurs still live. Doyle actually liked Challenger more than he liked Sherlock Holmes.

In many ways, Doyle was as much a man of action as Holmes or Challenger. He directed a field hospital during the Boer War. He sent coded messages to British prisoners during World War I. And he even did a bit of amateur detective work.

The "Sir" in front of his name means that he was knighted. He received this honor for his heroic actions during the Boer War. Not very fond of titles, Doyle accepted his knighthood reluctantly. In one of Doyle's stories, Sherlock Holmes was offered a knighthood too. Holmes *did* turn it down.

Other works by Sir Arthur Conan Doyle:
"The Adventure of the Speckled Band," short story
The Hound of the Baskervilles, novel
The Lost World, novel
"The Red-Headed League," short story
"A Scandal in Bohemia," short story

ADVENTURE OF THE GERMAN STUDENT

WASHINGTON IRVING

VOCABULARY PREVIEW

Below is a list of words that appear in the story. Read the list and get to know the words before you start the story.

conceived—imagined; pictured
eloquence—skillful way with words; clear expression
enthusiastic—eager; spirited
eruption—outburst; overflow
eternity—everlasting life; heaven
faltering—unsure; wobbly
fiend—devil; evil spirit
frenzy—madness; rage; great excitement
ghoul—one who feeds on dead people; cannibal
haunted—stayed in; obsessed
humble—plain; simple
liberal—free-thinking; open-minded
monument—figure; symbol
ornament—jewelry; decoration
passionate—excited; overeager
prejudices—long-held beliefs or ideas
preying—burdening; weighing down
recess—corner
sacrificed—offered; given up
society—general public; humankind
superstitions—fears; false ideas

Adventure of the German Student

A student named Wolfgang has lost touch with the real world. He believes that his dearest dream has come true—and perhaps it has. But it turns out to be a nightmare.

It was a stormy night during the violent times of the French Revolution.[1] A young German was returning to his room at a late hour. He crossed the old part of Paris. The lightning gleamed. The loud claps of thunder rattled through the high, narrow streets. But let me first tell you something about this young German.

Gottfried Wolfgang was a young man of a good family. He had studied for some time at Göttingen,[2] but he was a dreamer and an **enthusiastic** type. So he had wandered into wild and strange beliefs. Such thoughts have often confused other German students.

[1] In the French Revolution, which began in 1789, common people rebelled against the French nobility and the church.

[2] (gər'-tin-ən) Göttingen, Germany, is famous for its university, which was founded in the 1730s.

Wolfgang was lonely, and he worked very hard. His studies were unusual in nature. All of that affected both mind and body. In fact, his health was damaged, and his imagination was diseased. Strange spiritual ideas overtook him. Soon, like Swedenborg,[3] he had an ideal world of his own surrounding him.

He got the notion that there was an evil power hanging over him. I do not know what caused this idea. He thought that an evil spirit, or **fiend,** was trying to trap him—to make certain that his soul was lost.

Such an idea working on his unhappy nature produced the most gloomy effects. He became sickly and sad. His friends discovered the mental illness **preying** upon him. They decided that the best cure was a change of scenery. He was sent, therefore, to finish his studies among the wonders and joys of Paris.

Wolfgang arrived in Paris at the beginning of the revolution. At first, the popular madness caught his enthusiastic mind. He was delighted with the political and philosophical ideas[4] of the day. But the scenes of blood that followed shocked his sensitive nature. He became disgusted with **society** and the world. This made him withdraw from the world more than ever.

He shut himself up in a lonely apartment in the Latin Quarter, the part of the city where students lived. It was a gloomy street, not far from the scholarly walls of the Sorbonne.[5] There he pursued his beliefs.

Sometimes he spent hours at a time in the great libraries of Paris. They were like catacombs[6] of departed authors. He dug through their piles of dusty and out-of-date works. He searched for food for his unhealthy appetite. He was, in a way, a literary **ghoul.** He fed in the charnel-house[7] of decayed literature.

Wolfgang, though lonely and alone, was of a fiery nature. For a time, this trait affected his imagination. He

[3]Emanuel Swedenborg (1688–1772) was a Swedish scientist and theologian.
[4]The slogan of the French Revolution was "Liberty, Equality, Fraternity."
[5]The Sorbonne is a university in Paris.
[6]Catacombs are underground tunnels often used for burying the dead.
[7]A charnel-house is a building or room in which the bones or bodies of the dead are placed.

was too shy and ignorant of the world to make any advances to the ladies.

But he was a **passionate** admirer of female beauty. In his lonely room, he would often lose himself in dreams about the many forms and faces he had seen. He **conceived** images of loveliness far greater than the real ones.

While his mind was in this excited and weakened state, he had a dream. He dreamed of a female face of perfect beauty. So strong was its effect upon him that he dreamed of it again and again. It **haunted** his thoughts by day and his sleep by night. In short, he fell passionately in love with this shadow of a dream.

This lasted a very long time. It became one of those fixed ideas that haunt the minds of gloomy men. Such things are at times mistaken for madness.

Such was Gottfried Wolfgang. And such was his life at the time I mentioned. He was returning home late one stormy night. He went through some of the old and gloomy streets of the Marais,[8] the ancient part of Paris.

The loud claps of thunder rattled among the high houses of the narrow streets. He came to the Place de Grève, the square where public executions were performed. The lightning trembled around the peaks of the ancient building behind the square. It shed flickering gleams over the open space in front.

As Wolfgang was crossing the square, he shrank back in horror. He had found himself close to the guillotine. This dreadful tool of death stood ever ready. Its scaffold[9] was always running with the blood of the good and the brave. It had, that very day, been actively used in the work of murder. And there it stood in grim display. In a silent, sleeping city, it waited for fresh victims.

Wolfgang's heart grew sick within him. He turned, shuddering, from the horrible engine. Then he saw a shadowy form. It cowered at the foot of the steps that led up to the scaffold.

[8]The Marais district is across the Seine River from the Latin Quarter.
[9]A scaffold is a platform used in an execution.

A series of bright flashes of lightning revealed it more clearly. It was a female figure, dressed in black. She was seated on one of the lower steps of the scaffold. She leaned forward, and her face was hidden in her lap. Her long hair hung to the ground, tangled and streaming with the rain that poured down.

Wolfgang paused. There was something awful in this lonely **monument** of grief. The female had the look of being above the common class. Wolfgang knew the times to be full of change. Many a fair head that had once slept on a soft pillow now wandered the streets without a home.

Perhaps this was some poor mourner who had been made lonely by the ax. Perhaps she sat here heartbroken. Perhaps all that was dear to her had been sent into **eternity.**

He approached the woman and spoke to her in tones of sympathy. She raised her head and gazed wildly at him. He was filled with amazement at the face he saw by the bright glare of the lightning. It was the very face that had haunted him in his dreams. It was pale and unhappy, but thrillingly beautiful.

Trembling with violent and confusing emotions, Wolfgang spoke to her again. He said something about her being unprotected at such an hour of the night. He spoke of the fury of the storm and offered to lead her to her friends. She pointed to the guillotine with a gesture of dreadful meaning.

"I have no friend on earth!" she said.

"But you have a home," said Wolfgang.

"Yes—in the grave!"

The heart of the student melted at the words.

"May a stranger dare make an offer," he said, "without danger of being misunderstood? I would offer my **humble** dwelling as a shelter and myself as a devoted friend. I am friendless in Paris and a stranger in the land. If my life could be of service, it is at your command. It would be **sacrificed** before harm or insult could come to you."

There was an honest seriousness in the young man's manner that had its effect. His foreign accent, too, was in his favor. It showed him not to be the usual native of Paris. Indeed, there is an **eloquence** in true enthusiasm that cannot be doubted. The homeless stranger turned herself over completely to the protection of the student.

He supported her **faltering** steps across the Pont Neuf.[10] They passed the place where the statue of Henry the Fourth[11] had been thrown down by the people. The storm had let up, and the thunder rumbled at a distance. All Paris was quiet. That great volcano of human passion slept for a while. It gathered fresh strength for the next day's **eruption.**

The student led the woman through the ancient streets of the Latin Quarter. He took her by the dark walls of the Sorbonne to the great dingy hotel where he lived. The old woman doorkeeper who admitted them stared with surprise. It was an unusual sight to see the gloomy Wolfgang with a female companion.

They entered his apartment. The student blushed at his bare and ordinary home. He had only one room—an old-fashioned living room. It had heavy, carved woodwork, and it was crazily furnished with the remains of former glory.

This was one of those hotels in the area of the Luxembourg Palace[12] that had once belonged to nobility. It was filled with books and papers and all the usual junk of a student. His bed stood in a **recess** at one end.

When the lanterns were lit, the student had a better chance to see the stranger. He was positively drunk with her beauty. Her face was pale, but of a dazzling fairness. It was set off by full raven hair that clustered about it. Her large, bright eyes had an unusual, almost wild expression.

As much as her black dress permitted her shape to be seen, her figure was of perfect balance. Her whole appearance was highly striking, though she was dressed in

[10]The Pont Neuf is a bridge across the Seine.
[11]Henry the Fourth reigned as France's king from 1589 to 1610.
[12]Luxembourg Palace was once a royal home.

the simplest style. She wore only one thing close to an **ornament.** That was a broad black band with a diamond clasp around her neck.

The student now became perplexed about how to take care of the helpless being thus thrown upon his protection. He thought of leaving his room to her and seeking shelter elsewhere. Still, he was fascinated by her charms. There seemed to be a spell upon his thoughts and senses. He could not tear himself away from her presence.

Her manner, too, was unusual and unexplained. She spoke no more of the guillotine. Her grief had stopped. The student's care had first won her trust. Then he had apparently won her heart. She seemed to be an enthusiastic type like he was. And such people soon understand each other.

In the emotion of the moment, Wolfgang vowed his passion for her. He told her the story of his mysterious dream. He said that she had possessed his heart before he had ever seen her. She was strangely moved by his speech. She admitted to having felt drawn to him just as mysteriously.

It was a time for wild theory and wild actions. Old **prejudices** and **superstitions** were done away with. Everything was now under the rule of the "Goddess of Reason."[13] Among other rubbish of the old times were the forms and ceremonies of marriage. They were considered too many ties for honorable minds. Social agreements were the style. Wolfgang was too much of a thinker to not be affected by the **liberal** beliefs of the day.

"Why should we separate?" asked Wolfgang. "Our hearts are united. In the eye of reason and honor, we are as one. What need is there of earthly forms to bind high souls together?"

The stranger listened with feeling. She must have been taught at the same school of thought.

"You have no home or family," he continued. "Let me

---

[13]During the Reign of Terror, even the most violent acts were carried out in the name of reason.

be everything to you. Or, rather, let us be everything to one another. If form is necessary, form shall be observed—there is my hand. I pledge myself to you forever."

"Forever?" asked the stranger, solemnly.

"Forever!" repeated Wolfgang.

The stranger clasped the hand held out to her. "Then I am yours," she murmured, and she sank upon his chest.

The next morning, the student left his bride sleeping. He set out at an early hour to seek more spacious apartments. He wanted something suitable to the change in his life. When he returned, he found the stranger lying with her head and one arm hanging over the bed.

He spoke to her, but he received no reply. He went to wake her from her uneasy position. When he took her hand, it was cold—there was no pulse. Her face was pale and horrible. In a word, she was a corpse.

Horrified and frantic, he called for help to everyone in the house. A scene of confusion followed. The police were sent for. As the police officer entered the room, he jumped back on seeing the corpse.

"Great heaven!" he cried. "How did the woman come here?"

"Do you know anything about her?" asked Wolfgang eagerly.

"Do I!" cried the officer. "She was guillotined yesterday."

He stepped forward. He undid the black collar around the neck of the corpse, and the head rolled onto the floor!

The student burst into a **frenzy.** "The fiend! The fiend has gained possession of me!" he shrieked. "I am lost forever."

They tried to soothe Wolfgang, but it was in vain. He was taken with a frightful belief. He was sure that an evil spirit had brought the dead body back to life to trap him. He went insane and died in a madhouse.

INSIGHTS INTO WASHINGTON IRVING

(1783–1859)

Washington Irving practiced law for a time before devoting himself to writing full-time. He became one of the first American authors to achieve critical success in Europe as well as the United States.

While still in his twenties, Irving was engaged to a young woman named Matilda Hoffman. Matilda died before reaching the age of eighteen. Irving never married—in fact, he mourned his fiancée for the rest of his life. And after Matilda's death, he became more serious about his writing career.

Irving was a pioneer of the short story. Today he is best remembered for "The Legend of Sleepy Hollow" and "Rip Van Winkle." The latter is about a man who falls asleep in the woods and wakes up twenty years later. He has trouble adjusting to all the changes that have happened in America.

Later in life, Irving went through a similar experience. He once spent seventeen years in Europe without coming home to America. When at last he *did* return, America was quite changed, indeed! New York City, for example, had become more fast-paced and hard-edged. Irving felt very much like Rip Van Winkle.

Irving made many interesting contributions to American life, some of which aren't literary. When he was young, Americans did not celebrate Christmas. Then Irving published several stories about life in England. Some of them described how the English celebrated Christmas. Americans were charmed by the idea, and Christmas has been celebrated here ever since.

Other works by Washington Irving:
"The Devil and Tom Walker," short story
"The Legend of Sleepy Hollow," short story
"Rip Van Winkle," short story

THE BODY-SNATCHER

ROBERT LOUIS STEVENSON

VOCABULARY PREVIEW

Below is a list of words that appear in the story. Read the list and get to know the words before you start the story.

ambitious—determined; working toward a goal
anatomy—study of the human body
conscience—sense of right and wrong; principles
desecrate—disturb; dishonor
dissected—cut apart; closely examined
exuded—gave off
fate—life; outcome; luck
haste—speed; promptness
immoral—without goodness; sinful
instinctively—automatically; naturally
morality—goodness of character
mortality—death
precious—valuable; prized
prophecy—prediction; statement about the future
recoiled—flinched; pulled back
resurrection—rebirth; revival
ruffians—tough characters; hoodlums
temptation—attraction; lure
vanity—pride; ego

The Body-Snatcher

Medical students have dissected human bodies for centuries. But for a very long time, there was no way to get such bodies. Digging them up from graveyards was profitable but illegal. And sometimes, the body-snatchers resorted to murder.

Every night of the year, four of us sat in the small parlor[1] of the George Inn at Debenham.[2] There was the undertaker and the landlord and Fettes and myself. Sometimes there would be more. But blow high, blow low, come rain or snow or frost, we four would be there. Each would be planted in his own particular armchair.

Fettes was an old drunken Scotchman. He was clearly a man of education. He was also a man with family money, since he never did any work. He had come to Debenham years ago, while still young. Merely by continuing to live there, he had become a townsman.

His blue wool cloak was as familiar to everyone as the church spire.[3] His place in the parlor at the George and his absence from church were taken for granted in Debenham. So were all of his shabby, drunken ill deeds.

[1] A parlor is a sitting room for conversation.
[2] Debenham is a town in England, northeast of London.
[3] A spire is a steeple. It's a tall point on a church roof.

He had some unclear and extreme opinions and some small disloyalties. Now and again he would speak of them and drive them home with tottering slaps upon the table. He drank rum regularly—five glasses every evening. For the greater part of his nightly visit to the George, he just sat with his glass in his right hand. He was usually in a state of sadness and alcoholic fullness.

We called him "the doctor" because he supposedly had some special knowledge of medicine. He had been known, in a pinch, to set a fracture or reduce a dislocation. But beyond these slight details, we had no knowledge of who he was or where he had come from.

One dark winter night, the landlord joined us after it had struck nine. There was a sick man in the George. A great neighboring landowner had been struck down with a fit on his way to Parliament.[4]

The great man's still greater London doctor had been telegraphed to his bedside. Because the railway had just opened, it was the first time that such a thing had happened in Debenham. We were all suitably moved by the occurrence.

"He's come," said the landlord after filling and lighting his pipe.

"He?" said I. "Who? Not the doctor?"

"Himself," replied our host.

"What is his name?"

"Dr. Macfarlane," said the landlord.

Fettes was far through his third glass, stupidly confused. He was nodded over and stared dully around him. But at the last word, he seemed to awaken. He repeated Macfarlane's name twice, quietly the first time. But he showed sudden emotion at the second.

"Yes," answered the landlord. "That's his name, Dr. Wolfe Macfarlane."

Fettes suddenly became sober. His eyes opened fully. His voice became clear, loud, and steady. His language became forceful and serious. We were all startled by this

[4]Parliament is the British lawmaking branch of the government.

instant change. It was as if the man had risen from the dead.

"I beg your pardon," Fettes said. "I am afraid I have not been paying much attention to your talk. Who is this Wolfe Macfarlane?" And then, when he had heard the landlord out, he added, "It cannot be, it cannot be. And yet I would like very much to see him face to face."

"Do you know him, doctor?" gasped the undertaker.

"God forbid!" was the reply. "And yet the name is a strange one. It's too much to imagine two of them. Tell me, landlord, is he old?"

"Well," said the host, "he's not a young man, to be sure. His hair is white. But he looks younger than you."

"He is older though. Years older. It's the rum you see in my face," said Fettes with a slap upon the table. "Rum and sin. This other man may have a healthy stomach and an easy **conscience**—conscience! Hear me speak! You would think I was some decent old Christian, wouldn't you? But no, not I. I never pretended to be religious. Voltaire[5] might have done so had he stood in my shoes. But my brains," he said with a rattling rap on his bald head, "my brains were clear and active. I saw and made no judgments."

After an awful pause, I remarked, "If you know this doctor, I gather that you do not share the landlord's good opinion."

Fettes paid no regard to me.

"Yes," he said, with sudden decision. "I must see him face to face."

There was another pause, and then a door closed rather sharply on the first floor.[6] A step was heard upon the stair.

"That's the doctor!" cried the landlord. "Look sharp and you can catch him."

It was but two steps from the small parlor to the door of the old George Inn. The wide oak staircase landed almost in the street. There was room for a Turkish rug

[5]Voltaire was a French author.
[6]In England, the first floor is the first one above the ground floor.

and nothing more between the bottom of the staircase and the front of the inn.

There was a light upon the stair and a great signal-lamp below the sign. The warm glow of the barroom window lit up the area too. That was how the George brightly displayed itself to those who passed by in the cold street.

Fettes walked steadily to the spot. We were hanging behind. We saw the two men meet—face to face, as one of them had put it.

Dr. Macfarlane was alert and vigorous. His white hair set off his pale, calm face. He was dressed in the finest of broadcloth and the whitest of linen. He wore a great gold watch chain. His buttons and spectacles were of the same **precious** material. He wore a broad, folded tie that was white and speckled with lilac. He carried on his arm a comfortable driving coat of fur. There was no doubt that he looked good for his years. He **exuded** wealth and comfort.

By contrast, Fettes was bald, dirty, pimpled, and robed in his old wool cloak. It was a surprise to see our old parlor drunk meet the doctor at the bottom of the stairs.

"Macfarlane!" Fettes said rather loudly. He sounded more like an announcer than a friend.

The great doctor stopped short on the fourth step. The familiarity of the greeting seemed to surprise him and somewhat shock his dignity.

"Toddy Macfarlane!" repeated Fettes.

The London man almost staggered. He stared, for the swiftest of seconds, at the man before him. He glanced behind him with alarm. Then, in a startled whisper, he said, "Fettes—you!"

"Ay," said the other. "Me. Did you think I was dead too? We are not so easily finished with our friendship."

"Hush, hush!" exclaimed the doctor. "Hush, hush! This meeting is so unexpected. I can see that you are shaken and upset. I confess that I hardly knew you at first. But I am overjoyed—overjoyed to have this chance.

But for now," he continued, "it must be how-do-you-do and good-bye in one. My coach is waiting, and I must not miss the train. But you shall—let me see—yes—you shall give me your address. You can count on early news from me. We must do something for you, Fettes. I fear you have fallen on bad times. We must take care of that for *auld lang syne.*"[7]

"Money!" cried Fettes. "Money from you! The money that I had from you is lying where I cast it in the rain."

While talking, Dr. Macfarlane had become very sure of himself. Then the unusual energy of this refusal cast him back into confusion.

A horrible, ugly look came and went across his almost honorable features. "My dear fellow," he said, "be it as you please. My last thought is to anger you. I don't want to bother anyone. I will leave you my address, however—"

"I do not wish it," interrupted Fettes. "I do not wish to know the roof that shelters you. I heard your name. I feared it might be you. I wished to know if there were a God. I know now that there is none. Begone!"

Fettes stood still in the middle of the rug, which was between the stair and doorway. In order to escape, the great London physician would be forced to step to one side. It was plain that he paused at the thought of losing face like this.

White as the doctor was, there was a dangerous glitter in his glasses. While he hesitated, he became aware of the driver of his coach. The driver was peering in from the street at this unusual scene. At the same time, the doctor caught a glimpse of our little group from the parlor. We were huddled by the corner of the bar.

The presence of so many witnesses convinced the doctor to flee. He crouched, brushing against the wall panels. He made a dart like a snake, striking for the door. But his trouble was not yet entirely over. Even as Macfarlane was passing, Fettes clutched him by the arm. These words came in a painfully clear whisper: "Have you

[7] *Auld lang syne* is Scottish for "the good old days."

seen it again?"

The great London doctor cried out with a sharp, choking cry. He forced his questioner across the open space. With his hands over his head, the doctor fled out the door like a caught thief. Before it had occurred to one of us to make a movement, the coach was already rattling toward the station.

The scene was over like a dream. But the dream had left proofs and traces of its passage. The next day, the servant found the fine gold glasses broken just outside. That very night, we were all standing breathless by the barroom window. Fettes was at our side. He was sober, pale, and looking hard.

The landlord was the first of us to come back to his usual senses. "God protect us, Mr. Fettes!" he said. "What in the universe is all this? These are strange things you have been saying."

Fettes turned toward us. He looked us each in turn in the face. "See if you can hold your tongues," he said. "That man Macfarlane is not safe to cross. Those that have done so already have been sorry for it too late."

Then, without even finishing his third glass, Fettes bade us good-bye. And he went out into the black night.

We three returned to our places in the parlor. We went over what had happened. Then the first chill of our surprise changed into a glow of curiosity. We sat up late. It was the latest session I have known in the old George.

Each man had his opinion that he was set to prove. And none of us had any more important business in this world than to figure out the past of our unhappy friend. We wanted to discover the secret that he shared with the great London doctor.

It is no great boast, but I believe that I was a better hand at worming out a story than either of my fellows at the George. Perhaps there is now no other man alive who could tell you the following foul and unnatural events.

In his young days, Fettes studied medicine in the schools of Edinburgh.[8] He had a talent of a kind. His was the skill that picks up swiftly what it hears and readily sells it for what it's worth.

He worked little at home. But he was polite, thoughtful, and intelligent in the presence of his masters. They soon picked him out as a lad who listened closely and remembered well. Strange as it seemed to me, he was well thought of in those days. They were pleased by his appearance.

There was, then, a certain special teacher of **anatomy.** I shall call him here by the letter K. His name was later quite known. The man who bore it once sneaked through the streets of Edinburgh in disguise. That was while the mob that applauded at the execution of Burke[9] called loudly for the blood of his employer.

But Mr. K—— was then at the top of his fame. He enjoyed a popularity due partly to his own talent and social abilities and partly to the stupidity of his rival, the university professor. The students, at least, swore by Mr. K——'s name. Fettes believed that he had laid the groundwork for success when he gained the favor of this brilliantly famous man. Others believed so too.

Mr. K—— was a *bon vivant*[10] as well as an excellent teacher. He liked a student who could fool people as well as one who was knowledgeable in his studies. In both ways, Fettes enjoyed and deserved his notice. By the second year of his attendance, Fettes held the half-time position of second demonstrator, or sub-assistant,[11] in his class.

In this job, the charge of the theatre[12] and lecture room fell upon his shoulders. He was responsible for the cleanliness of the place and the conduct of the other students.

[8]Edinburgh is the capital of Scotland.
[9]William Burke (1792–1829) was hanged in Edinburgh for murdering at least 15 people, digging up corpses, and selling their bodies for dissection.
[10]*Bon vivant* is a French phrase, meaning "one who lives well."
[11]Demonstrators and assistants helped professors.
[12]"Theatre" here refers to a large room where surgeries or dissections are performed in front of students.

It was a part of his duty to find, receive, and divide the human subjects for dissection. Because of this last matter, Fettes was housed by Mr. K——. His room was on the same narrow street, and later in the same building with the dissecting rooms.

Here, after a night of rough pleasures, Fettes' hand would still be shaking. His sight would still be misty and confused. He would be called out of bed in the black hours before the winter dawn. He would be awakened by the unclean and desperate strangers who supplied the table.

Fettes would open the door to these men, who were later hated throughout the land. He would help them with their tragic weight and pay their evil price. When they were gone, he would remain alone with the unfriendly remains of human beings.

From such a scene, he would return to snatch another hour or two of slumber. He slept to get over the night's drinking and to refresh himself for the labors of the day.

Few lads could have been more unfeeling of the effects of a life thus passed among the signs of **mortality.** His mind was closed against all normal concerns. He had no interest in the **fate** of anyone else. He was a slave to his own desires and low purposes.

Fettes was cold, light, and selfish in every way. He had that bit of caution that keeps a man from being caught at drunkenness or punishable theft. It is often mistaken for **morality.**

And he desired a certain amount of respect from his masters and fellow pupils. He had no desire to fail so that everyone could see it. Thus, he made it his goal to gain some notice in his studies.

Day after day, he worked hard—to the complete satisfaction of his employer, Mr. K——. He rewarded himself for his days of work with nights of rowdy enjoyment. When that balance was struck, his conscience told him that it was content.

The short supply of subjects was always trouble to him as well as to his master. In that large and busy class, the raw material needed by the anatomists kept running out. And the necessary business that resulted was more than just unpleasant—it threatened dangerous results to all who were involved.

It was Mr. K——'s habit to ask no questions in his dealings with the trade. "They bring the body, and we pay the price," he used to say. And he would add—"*quid pro quo.*"[13] Then, to his assistants, he would say wickedly, "Ask no questions, for conscience's sake."

There was no thought that the subjects were provided by the crime of murder. Had that idea been suggested to him in words, Mr. K—— would have **recoiled** in horror. But the thought was a **temptation** to the men with whom he dealt.

Fettes, for instance, had often noticed the unusual freshness of the bodies. And he observed the horrible hang-dog looks of the **ruffians** who brought the bodies to him before the dawn. He had put things together clearly in his private thoughts. Perhaps he had even found wicked and **immoral** meanings in the unguarded words of his master. But even so, Fettes understood that he had three duties. He was to take what was brought. He was to pay the price. And he was to turn his eye from any sign of crime.

One November morning, this rule of silence was put to the test. He had been awake all night with a painful toothache. He had paced his room like a caged beast and thrown himself in fury on the bed. At last, he had fallen into that deep, uneasy slumber that so often follows a night of pain.

Fettes was awakened when the double knock on his door was repeated for the third or fourth time. There was a thin, bright moonshine. It was bitter cold, windy, and frosty. The town had not yet awakened, but the noise and business of the day had already started to stir. The hoodlums

[13]*Quid pro quo* is Latin for "something for something."

had come later than usual, and they seemed more than usually eager to be gone.

Fettes, sick with sleep, lighted their way upstairs. He heard their grumbling Irish voices through a dream. As they stripped the sack from their sad package, Fettes leaned, dozing, with his shoulder propped against the wall. He had to shake himself to find the money for the men. As he did so, his eyes fell upon the dead face. He started. He took two steps nearer and raised the candle.

"God Almighty!" he cried. "That is Jane Galbraith!"

The men did not answer, but they shuffled nearer the door.

"I know her, I tell you," Fettes continued. "She was alive and hearty yesterday. It is impossible for her to be dead. You could not have gotten this body fairly."

"Surely, sir, you're mistaken entirely," said one of the men.

But the other looked Fettes darkly in the eyes and demanded the money on the spot.

It was impossible to mistake the threat or to make too much of the danger. The lad's heart failed him. He stammered some excuse, counted out the sum, and saw his hateful visitors depart.

No sooner were they gone than Fettes hurried to confirm his doubts. By a dozen unquestionable features, he made sure that she was the girl he had joked with the day before. Horrified, he saw many marks upon her body that might well have indicated violence.

A panic seized him, and he hid in his room. He thought at length about the discovery he had made. He soberly considered the bearing of Mr. K——'s instructions and the danger to himself of meddling in such serious business. At last, in great confusion, Fettes decided to wait for the advice of the person who ranked above him. This was the class assistant.

The class assistant was Wolfe Macfarlane, a young doctor, who was a high favorite among all the reckless students. He was clever, wicked, and crooked to the last degree.

Macfarlane had traveled and studied abroad. His manners were agreeable and a little forward. He was an expert on the stage. He was skillful with a skate on the ice or a golf club in the field. And he dressed with just enough daring. To put the finishing touch upon his glory, he kept a gig[14] and a strong horse.

With Fettes, Macfarlane was on familiar terms. Indeed, the jobs they had to do called for some fellow-ship. When subjects were scarce, the pair would drive far into the country in Macfarlane's gig. They would visit and **desecrate** some lonely graveyard. Then they would return before dawn with their loot to the door of the dissecting room.

On that particular morning, Macfarlane arrived some-what earlier than usual. Fettes heard him and met him on the stairs. He told him his story and showed him the cause of his alarm. Macfarlane examined the marks on her body.

"Yes," he said with a nod. "It looks fishy."

"What should I do?" asked Fettes.

"Do?" repeated the other. "Do you want to do any-thing? Least said, soonest mended. That's what I say."

"Someone else might recognize her," objected Fettes. "She was as well known as the Castle Rock."[15]

"Let's hope not," said Macfarlane. "And if anybody does—well, you didn't, don't you see. And there's an end to it. The fact is, this has been going on too long. Stir up the mud, and you'll get K—— into the most unholy trou-ble. You'll be in a shocking fix yourself. So will I, if it comes to that.

"I should like to know how any one of us would look. What the devil would we have to say for ourselves in any Christian courtroom? As far as I'm concerned, one thing is certain. Just about all of our subjects have been mur-dered."

"Macfarlane!" cried Fettes.

[14]A gig is a light, two-wheeled, one-horse carriage.
[15]Edinburgh Castle sits upon Castle Rock.

"Come now!" sneered Macfarlane. "As if you hadn't suspected it yourself!"

"Suspecting is one thing—"

"And proof another. Yes, I know. And I'm as sorry as you are that this should have come here." He tapped the body with his cane. "The next best thing for me is not to recognize it. And I don't," he added coolly. "You may, if you please. I don't want to tell you what to do. But I think a man of the world would do as I do. And, I may add, I imagine that K—— would expect us to do the same. The question is, why did he choose the two of us for his assistants? I would answer that he chose us because he didn't want tattle-tales."

This was the tone, above all others, to affect the mind of a lad like Fettes. He agreed to do just as Macfarlane did. The body of the unlucky girl was duly **dissected**. No one noticed or appeared to recognize her.

One afternoon, when his day's work was over, Fettes dropped into a popular tavern. There he found Macfarlane sitting with a stranger. This was a small man, very pale and dark, with coal-black eyes. The shape of his face gave a promise of intellect and good manners. But those were only feebly present in his actions. He proved, when one got to know him, to be coarse, vulgar, and stupid. However, the man held a very remarkable control over Macfarlane. He issued orders like the Great Bashaw.[16] He became enraged at the least discussion or delay. And he commented rudely on how easily he was obeyed.

This most unpleasant person took a fancy to Fettes on the spot. He bought Fettes many drinks and honored him with unusual secrets of his own past career. If a tenth part of what he confessed was true, he was a very nasty villain. The lad's **vanity** was tickled by the attention of such an experienced man.

"I'm a pretty bad fellow myself," the stranger remarked. "But Macfarlane is the boy. Toddy Macfarlane,

[16]"Great Bashaw" is a term for an arrogant, domineering man.

I call him. Toddy, order your friend another glass." Or it might be, "Toddy, jump up and shut the door." And he said, over and over, "Toddy hates me. Oh yes, Toddy, you do!"

"Don't call me that blasted name," growled Macfarlane.

"Hear him! Did you ever see the lads play with knives? He would like to do that all over my body," remarked the stranger.

"We medicals have a better way than that," said Fettes. "When we dislike a dreadful friend of ours, we dissect him."

Macfarlane looked up sharply, as though this jest was not to his liking.

The afternoon passed. The stranger, whose name was Gray, invited Fettes to join them at dinner. He ordered a feast so fine that the tavern was thrown into an uproar. And when all was done, he commanded Macfarlane to settle the bill.

It was late before they separated. Gray was badly drunk, but Macfarlane was sobered by his fury. He thought about the money he had been forced to spend and the insults he had been made to swallow. Fettes had many liquors singing in his head. He returned home with crooked footsteps and a mind that was entirely blank.

The next day, Macfarlane was absent from the class. Fettes smiled to himself. He imagined Macfarlane still going with the awful Gray from tavern to tavern. As soon as the hour of liberty had struck, Fettes hurried from place to place in search of his last night's companions. But he could find them nowhere. He returned wearily to his rooms, went early to bed, and slept the sleep of the just.

At four in the morning, he was awakened by the well-known signal. Rushing to the door, he was filled with amazement to find Macfarlane with his gig. In the gig was one of those long and ghastly packages he knew so well.

"What?" he cried. "Have you been out alone? How did you manage?"

But Macfarlane silenced him roughly, telling him to turn to business. They got the body upstairs and laid it on the table. Macfarlane acted at first as if he was going away. Then he paused and seemed uncertain.

"You should look at the face," he said in a controlled tone. "You had better," he repeated. Fettes only stared at him in wonder.

"But where, and how, and when did you come by it?" cried Fettes.

"Look at the face," was the only answer.

Fettes was staggered. Strange doubts assailed him. He looked from the young doctor to the body and then back again. At last, he did as he was told. He had almost expected the sight that met his eyes, and yet the shock was cruel.

The sight awoke, even in the thoughtless Fettes, some of the terrors of the conscience. Fixed in the stiffness of death and naked on that coarse layer of the cloth sack was a man he knew. It was the man whom he had left fully dressed and full of meat and sin just outside a tavern.

Two people he had known had come to lie upon these icy tables. He found himself wondering who would be next.

Yet these thoughts were not at the top of his mind. His first concern was Macfarlane. Unprepared for a challenge so great, he could not look him in the face. He dared not meet his eye, and he had neither words nor voice at his command.

It was Macfarlane himself who made the first move. He came up quietly behind and laid his hand gently but firmly on Fettes' shoulder.

"Richardson," he said, "may have the head."

Richardson was a student who had long been eager to dissect that portion of the human body. There was no answer, and the murderer went on, "Talking of business, you must pay me. Your accounts, you see, must tally."

Fettes found a voice, the ghost of his own. "Pay you!" he cried. "Pay you for that?"

"Why, yes, of course you must. By all means and for every possible reason, you must," replied Macfarlane. "I dare not give it for nothing. You dare not take it for nothing. It would get us both into trouble. This is another case like Jane Galbraith's. The more things are wrong, the more we must act as if all were right. Where does old K—— keep his money?"

"There," answered Fettes hoarsely, pointing to a cupboard in the corner.

"Give me the key, then," said the other calmly, holding out his hand.

There was an instant's pause, and then the key was given. Macfarlane could not keep in a sigh of great relief. He gave a nervous twitch upon feeling the key between his fingers. He opened the cupboard. He brought out pen and ink and a paper book that was in one drawer. From the funds in another drawer, he counted out the correct amount of money.

"Now look here," Macfarlane said. "There is the payment made. That's the first proof of your good faith—the first step toward your safety. You must now secure it by a second. Enter the payment in your book. Then you, for your part, may defy the devil."

For Fettes, the next few seconds were complete torture. As he weighed terrors, the first one that came to mind seemed most frightening. He preferred facing whatever other difficulties his future might present to quarreling with Macfarlane.

He set down the candle he had been carrying all this time. With a steady hand, he entered the date, the nature, and the amount of the agreement.

"And now," said Macfarlane, "it's only fair that you should pocket the profit. I've had my share already. By the way, I'm ashamed to speak of it, but there's a certain rule to follow in this case. When a man of the world falls into a bit of luck and has a few shillings extra in his pocket, he must be careful. No treating, no purchase of expensive schoolbooks, no squaring of old debts. Borrow, don't lend."

"Macfarlane," said Fettes, still hoarsely. "I have put my neck in a noose to please you."

"To please me?" cried Macfarlane. "Oh, come! You did, as near as I can see the matter, what you downright had to do in self-defense. Suppose I got into trouble. Where would you be then? This second little matter follows clearly from the first. Mr. Gray is just like the case of Miss Galbraith. You can't begin and then stop. If you begin, you must keep on beginning. That's the truth. No rest for the wicked."

A horrible sense of blackness and the falseness of fate seized hold upon the soul of the unhappy student. "My God!" he cried. "But what have I done? And when did I begin? To be made a class assistant—in the name of reason, where's the harm in that? Service wanted the position. Service might have gotten it. Would *he* be where *I* am now?"

"My dear fellow," said Macfarlane, "what a boy you are! What harm *has* come to you? What harm *can* come to you if you hold your tongue? Why, man, do you know what this life is? There are two kinds of people—the lions and the lambs. If you're a lamb, you'll come to lie upon these tables like Gray or Jane Galbraith. If you're a lion, you'll live and drive a horse like me, like K——. Like anyone in the world with any wit or courage.

"You're staggered at the beginning," Macfarlane continued. "But look at K——! My dear fellow, you're clever. You have nerve. I like you, and K——likes you. You were born to lead the hunt. And I'll tell you something more, on my honor and my experience of life. Soon you'll laugh at all these scarecrows like a high school boy at a funny play."

And with that, Macfarlane took his leave. He drove off in his gig to hide before daylight. Fettes was thus left alone with his regrets. He saw the miserable danger in which he stood. He saw, with horrible dismay, that there was no limit to his weakness. And he saw how, from one bad move to the next, he had fallen.

Instead of becoming the judge of Macfarlane's destiny, Fettes had become his paid and helpless assistant. He would have given the world to have been a little braver when it had counted. But it did not occur to him that he might still be brave. The secret of Jane Galbraith and the cursed entry in the tally book closed his mouth.

Hours passed. The class began to arrive. The parts of the unhappy Gray were dealt out and received without remark. Richardson was happy to receive the head. Before the hour of freedom rang, Fettes trembled with delight to see how far they had already gone toward safety.

The dreadful game of hiding went on. For two days, Fettes continued to watch with an increasing joy.

On the third day, Macfarlane made his appearance. He had been ill, he said. But he made up for lost time by the energy with which he directed the students. To Richardson, in particular, Macfarlane extended the most valuable assistance and advice. Richardson was encouraged by the praise of the demonstrator. And, burning high with **ambitious** hopes, he saw his reward within his grasp.

Before the week was out, Macfarlane's **prophecy** had been fulfilled. Fettes had outlived his terrors and had forgotten his wickedness. He began to congratulate himself upon his courage. He had so arranged the story in his mind that he could look back on those events with an unhealthy pride.

He saw very little of Macfarlane. They met, of course, in the business of the class. They received their orders together from Mr. K——. And, at times, they had a word or two in private.

Macfarlane was always very kind and pleasant. But it was plain that he avoided any mention of their common secret. Fettes whispered to him that he had cast in his lot with the lions and given up the lambs. But Macfarlane only smiled and signaled to him to hold his peace.

At length, an occasion arose that threw the pair closer together. Mr. K—— was again short of subjects. Pupils were eager, and this teacher was always eager to look well supplied. The news of a burial in the country graveyard of Glencorse came at this time.

The graveyard stood then, as it does now, upon a crossroads out of hearing distance of human homes. It was buried far beneath the leaves of six cedar trees.

Only sheep cried upon the neighboring hills. Tiny streams were on either side. One sang loudly among pebbles; the other dripped quietly from pond to pond. The wind stirred in mountainous, old chestnut trees. And the voice of the bell and the tunes of the chorus were heard once every seventh day. These were the only sounds that disturbed the silence around the rural church.

The **Resurrection** Man[17]—to use a nickname of the period—was not to be stopped by anything sacred in common religion. It was part of his trade to spoil the scrolls and trumpets of old tombs. He would care nothing for the paths worn by the feet of worshippers and mourners. He would hate the offerings and the carvings of grieving love.

In country neighborhoods, love is uncommonly strong. Some bonds of blood or fellowship hold together the entire society of a parish.[18] The body-snatcher was far from being put off by those bonds. Instead, he was attracted to the ease and safety of the task.

These bodies had been laid in the earth in joyful hope of a far different awakening. But then came that hasty, lamp-lit, terror-haunted resurrection of the spade and pick. The coffin was forced and the shroud torn. The sad remains were thrown into a sack and rattled for hours on moonless roads. Finally, they were exposed to complete humiliation before a class of gaping boys.

Fettes and Macfarlane were like vultures that swoop upon a dying lamb. And they were to be let loose upon a grave in that quiet, green resting place!

---

[17] A Resurrection Man was someone who stole bodies from graves for medical students.
[18] A parish is an area served by one particular church.

A farmer's wife had lived for sixty years. She had been known for nothing but good butter and godly conversation. Now she was to be rooted from her grave at midnight.

She would be carried, naked and dead, to the faraway city that she had always honored with her Sunday's best. The place beside her family was to be empty until the crack of doom. Her innocent and almost holy limbs were to be exposed to the last curiosity of the student of anatomy.

Late one afternoon, the pair set forth. They were well wrapped in cloaks and furnished with a huge bottle. It rained without stopping—a cold, heavy, lashing rain. Now and again a puff of wind blew, but these sheets of falling water kept it down.

Bottle and all, it was a sad and silent drive as far as Penicuik. They were to spend the evening there. They stopped once to hide their tools in a thick bush close to the churchyard. Then they stopped at the Fisher's Tryst, the local inn, to have a toast before the kitchen fire, and they varied their nips of whisky with a glass of ale.

Finally, they reached their journey's end. The gig was housed. The horse was fed and comforted. And the two young doctors ate in a private room.

They sat down to the best dinner and the best wine the house offered. They enjoyed the lights, the fire, and the beating rain upon the window. Even the cold, strange work that lay before them added enjoyment to their meal. With every glass, their friendliness grew. Soon Macfarlane handed a little pile of gold to his companion.

"A favor between friends," he said. "These little give-and-takes ought to go back and forth as if we were lighting each other's pipes."

Fettes pocketed the money and echoed the thought. "You are a wise man!" he cried. "I was an ass until I knew you. Between you and K——, by the devil, you'll make a man of me!"

"Of course we shall," applauded Macfarlane. "A man? I tell you, it took a man to back me up the other morning. There are some big, brawling, forty-year-old cowards who would have turned sick at the look of the cursed thing. But not you. You kept your head. I watched you."

"And why not?" Fettes explained. "It was no affair of mine. There was nothing to gain on the one side but trouble. And on the other, I could count on your gratitude, don't you see?" And he slapped his pocket until the gold pieces rang.

Macfarlane felt a certain touch of alarm at these unpleasant words. He may have regretted that he had taught his young companion so successfully. But he had no time to say anything, for Fettes noisily continued in this boastful way.

"The great thing is not to be afraid, Macfarlane. Just between you and me, I don't want to hang—that's practical. But I was born not to care anything for whatever people say. Hell, God, devil, right, wrong, sin, crime, and all the old gallery of curiosities—they may frighten boys. But we men of the world think nothing of them. Here's to the memory of Gray!"

It was by this time growing late. The gig was brought around to the door with both lamps brightly shining. The young men had to pay their bill and take the road.

They announced that they were bound for Peebles. And they drove in that direction until they were clear of the last house of the town. Then they put out the lamps and returned upon their path to Glencorse.

There was no sound besides that of their own passing and the strong and constant pouring of the rain. It was pitch dark. Here and there, a white gate or a white stone in the wall guided them for a short space in the night. But for the most part, they went at a slow, almost crawling pace. They picked their way through the ghostly blackness to the sad and lonely place they looked for.

They reached the sunken woods that crossed the neighborhood of the burying grounds. It was so dark that it became necessary to re-light one of the gig's lanterns. Under the dripping trees, they were surrounded by huge, moving shadows. Thus, they reached the scene of their unholy work.

They were both experienced in such affairs, and both were powerful with the spade. After just twenty minutes of digging, they were rewarded by a dull rattle on the coffin lid. They now stood in the grave almost to their shoulders. They were close to the edge of the graveyard. And the gig lamp had been propped against a tree on the brink of a steep bank that led to the stream.

Suddenly, Macfarlane hurt his hand on a stone. He flung the stone carelessly above his head. Chance had taken a sure aim with the stone. There came a clang of broken glass, and night fell upon them once more. Dull and ringing sounds announced the fall of the lantern down the bank. It occasionally struck the trees. In its fall, the lantern shook loose a few stones, which rattled behind it into the depths of the ravine.

And then silence, like the night, began its power again. They strained their hearing as much as they could, but nothing could be heard. Nothing except the rain— which was either marching to the wind or steadily falling over miles of open country.

They were nearly at the end of their hated task. So they judged that it would be wise to complete it in the dark. They dug out the coffin and broke it open. Then they inserted the body in the dripping sack and carried it between them to the gig. One mounted to keep it in its place. The other took the horse by the mouth. He crept along by wall and bush until they reached the wider road by the Fisher's Tryst.

Here was a faint, scattered light, which they welcomed like daylight. They pushed the horse to a good pace and began to rattle along merrily toward the town.

They had both been wet to the skin during their work. Now the gig jumped among deep ruts. The thing that stood propped between them fell upon one and then the other. At every repetition of the horrid contact, each man

instinctively pushed it away with greater **haste.** This action, although natural, began to wear upon the nerves of the companions.

Macfarlane made some ill-favored joke about the farmer's wife, but it rang hollowly from his lips and was allowed to drop in silence. Still, their unnatural burden bumped from side to side. Sometimes the head would be laid, as if telling a secret, upon their shoulders. Sometimes the drenched sackcloth would flap icily about their faces.

A creeping chill began to possess Fettes' soul. He peered at the bundle. It seemed larger than at first. From all over the countryside, near and far, the farm dogs joined in their journey with tragic howls.

It grew and grew upon Fettes' mind that some unnatural miracle had happened. He thought that some nameless change had happened to the dead body. And he was sure that it was in fear of their unholy burden that the dogs were howling.

"For God's sake," he said, making a great effort to arrive at speech. "For God's sake, let's have a light!"

It seemed that Macfarlane had been affected in the same way. For, though he made no reply, he stopped the horse. He passed the reins to his companion, got down, and lit the remaining lamp. They had, by that time, gotten no farther than the crossroads down to Auchenclinny.

The rain still poured. It was no easy matter to make a light in such a world of wet and darkness. When at last the flickering blue flame had been passed to the wick, it began to grow and brighten. It shed a wide circle of misty light round the gig. Then it became possible for the two young men to see each other and the thing they had along with them.

The rain had shaped the rough sacking to the outlines of the body underneath. The head could be clearly seen apart from the body. The shoulders were plainly modeled. Something at once unearthly and human locked their eyes upon the ghastly companion of their drive.

For some time, Macfarlane stood motionless. Fettes felt a nameless dread, wrapped like a wet sheet about his body. It tightened the white skin upon his face.

A fear that was meaningless, a horror of what could not be, kept climbing to his brain. Another beat of the watch and he would have spoken. But his companion stopped him.

"That is not a woman," said Macfarlane in a hushed voice.

"It was a woman when we put her in," whispered Fettes.

"Hold that lamp," said Macfarlane. "I must see her face."

And as Fettes took the lamp, his companion untied the fastenings of the sack. He drew down the cover from the head. The light fell very clearly upon the dark, well-formed features and smooth-shaven cheeks. It was a familiar face, and it had often been beheld in dreams of both these young men.

A wild yell rang into the night. Each leaped from his own side into the roadway. The lamp fell, broke, and was put out. And the horse, terrified by this extraordinary noise, bounded toward Edinburgh at a gallop. The horse carried with it the sole occupant of the gig—the body of the dead and long-dissected Gray.

INSIGHTS INTO ROBERT LOUIS STEVENSON (1850–1894)

In 1832, the Anatomy Act made it legal to obtain bodies for medical study in Great Britain. Before then, graves were robbed and people were sometimes murdered. Such wicked deeds gave Robert Louis Stevenson hair-raising material for this story.

But "The Body-Snatcher" was hardly Robert Louis Stevenson's favorite among his own tales. It was far from it. After writing it, he set it aside for a couple of years. He thought it unworthy of being published. When it finally appeared in 1884, he refused to accept full payment from his publisher because he didn't think the story deserved it.

But Stevenson's opinion hasn't stopped generations of readers from being chilled by it. Writers are often wrong about their own work.

Stevenson suffered from ill health since childhood. But even so, he lived an exciting life that took him all over the world. His life was scarcely more adventurous than his fiction, though. He seemed to have a limitless imagination.

He claimed that some of his stories came to him in dreams. This was true of one of his most famous novels, *The Strange Case of Dr. Jekyll and Mr. Hyde.* In fact, Stevenson could take the simplest idea and turn it into a story. His most famous novel, *Treasure Island,* got its start when he drew a treasure map while playing with his stepson.

Stevenson died in the beautiful South Sea islands of Samoa. He became chief of the natives there, who buried him with honor on a mountaintop.

Other works by Robert Louis Stevenson:
A Child's Garden of Verses, poetry collection
Kidnapped, novel
The Strange Case of Dr. Jekyll and Mr. Hyde, novel
Treasure Island, novel

THE YELLOW WALLPAPER

CHARLOTTE PERKINS GILMAN

VOCABULARY PREVIEW

Below is a list of words that appear in the story. Read the list and get to know the words before you start the story.

absurd—ridiculous; peculiar
arbors—shelters of vines or branches
burden—heavy responsibility; trouble
contradictions—conflicts; clashes
depressing—saddening
fantasies—dreams; imaginings
humiliating—causing shame; degrading
hysterical—emotional; crazed
influence—effect; power
opposition—resistance; disagreement
perhaps—possibly; maybe
principle—basic rule; standard; method
reasonable—logical; open-minded; clear-headed
respected—well thought of; looked up to and admired
sensitive—easily upset; touchy; irritable
sprawling—stretched or spread out
stylish—fashionable; popular
symmetry—sameness; consistency; balance
whim—crazy idea or impulse

The Yellow Wallpaper

If the narrator of this story would only use proper self-control and common sense, her nervous problem would disappear. After all, that's what her husband, who is also a medical doctor, tells her. So she doesn't tell him about the dim shapes, creeping figures, and strangled heads that lurk behind the wallpaper in her bedroom. But what will she do when they try to put her behind the hideous paper?

John and I are mere ordinary people. It is rare that folks like us get to stay in a wonderful house for the summer.

A very old mansion, a family estate! I want to call it a haunted house—now *that* would be exciting and **stylish.** But it would be asking too much of fate!

Still, I will proudly say that there is something odd about it. Why else should it be rented so cheaply? And why has it stood empty for so long?

John laughs at me, of course, but one expects that in marriage.

John is strictly a no-nonsense man. He has no patience with faith and a great fear of superstition. He believes only in things that are felt and seen and put down in figures. He laughs openly at talk of anything else.

John is a doctor. And **perhaps** that is one reason I do not get well faster. (I would never say that to a living soul, of course. But this is merely dead paper, and a great relief to my mind.)

You see, he does not believe I am sick!

And what can I do?

When a highly **respected** physician is your own husband . . . When he assures friends and relatives that there is really nothing the matter with you . . . When he says you have a short-term problem with nerves—that you just tend to be a little emotional, a little **hysterical . . .** What are you to do?

My brother is also a highly respected physician. And he says the same thing.

So I take phosphates[1] and tonics[2] and journeys and air and exercise. And I am absolutely not allowed to "work" until I am well again.

Personally, I disagree with their ideas.

Personally, I believe I could do with some excitement and change. And the right kind of work would do me good.

But what am I to do?

I did write for a while in spite of them. Having to be so sly about it exhausts me a good deal. But if I don't hide it, I meet with heavy **opposition.**

I sometimes think it would improve my health to have less opposition. Surely I need more company, more to keep me occupied.

[1] A phosphate is a carbonated drink.
[2] A tonic is a medicine that is supposed to make one stronger and more energetic.

But John says the very worst thing I can do is to think about my health. And I confess that it always makes me feel bad when I do.

So I will let it alone and talk about the house.

It is the most beautiful place! It is quite alone, standing well back from the road, all of three miles from the village. It makes me think of English places that you read about. There are hedges and walls and gates that lock. And there are many separate little houses for the gardeners and people.

There is a delicious garden! I never saw such a garden—large and shady, full of boxwood-bordered paths. And the paths are lined with long grape-covered **arbors** with seats under them.

There were greenhouses too, but they have all fallen now.

There was some legal trouble, I believe. Something about the heir.[3] Anyhow, the place has been empty for years.

There is something strange about the house—I can feel it.

I even said so to John one moonlit evening. But he said that what I felt was a *draft,* and he shut the window.

I get so angry with John sometimes. I'm sure I never used to be this **sensitive.** I think it is due to this nervous problem of mine.

But John says if I feel so much, I am neglecting proper self-control. So I take pains to control myself—in front of him, at least. That makes me very tired.

I don't like our room one bit. I wanted the one downstairs that opened on the patio. It had roses all over the window and such pretty old-fashioned chintz curtains! But John would not hear of it.

He said there was only one window and not room for two beds. And there was no nearby room for him if he took another.

He is very careful and loving. He hardly lets me stir without special instructions.

[3]An heir is a person who receives the property of someone who has died.

I have a schedule worked out for each hour in the day. He takes all responsibility from me, so I feel terribly ungrateful not to value it more.

He said we came here just because of me. I was to have perfect rest and all the air I could get.

"Your exercise depends on your strength, my dear," he said. "And your food depends somewhat on your appetite. But you can breathe air all the time."

So we took the nursery at the top of the house.

It is a big, beautiful, airy room that nearly takes up the whole floor. It has windows that look all ways and lots of air and sunshine. It was a nursery first and then a playground and gymnasium, I believe. The windows are barred for little children. And there are rings and things in the walls.

The paint and paper look as if a boys' school had used it. The paper is stripped off in great patches all around the head of my bed. It is stripped off about as far as I can reach. And also in a great place on the other side of the room, low down. I never saw worse paper in my life.

It is one of those **sprawling,** flashy patterns that commit every artistic sin.

It is dull enough to confuse the eye. It is clear enough to constantly bother you but keep you looking at it. And when you follow the lame, uncertain curves for a little distance, they suddenly commit suicide. They plunge off at crazy angles. They destroy themselves in unheard-of **contradictions.**

The color is ugly, almost horrible—a smoky yellow. It is strangely faded by the slow-turning sunlight. It is a dull yet glowing orange in some places, a sickly sulfur color in others.

No wonder the children hated it! I should hate it myself if I had to live in this room long.

Here comes John, and I must put this away. He hates to have me write a word.

*   *   *

We have been here two weeks. I haven't felt like writing since that first day.

I am sitting by the window now, up in the horrible nursery. There is nothing except lack of strength to prevent my writing as much as I please.

John is away all day. Even some nights when his cases are serious.

I am glad my case is not serious!

But these nervous troubles are dreadfully **depressing.**

John does not know how much I really suffer. He knows there is no *reason* to suffer, and that satisfies him.

Of course, it is only nervousness. It does weigh on me so not to do my duty in any way! I meant to be such a help to John, such a real rest and comfort. And here I am turning into a **burden** already!

Nobody would believe what an effort it is to do what little I am able—to dress and entertain and order things.

It is fortunate that Mary is so good with the baby. Such a dear baby! And yet I *cannot* be with him, it makes me so nervous.

I suppose John never was nervous in his life. He laughs at me so about this wallpaper!

At first, he planned to re-paper the room. But he said afterward that I was letting it get the better of me. He said nothing was worse for a nervous patient than to give way to such ideas.

He said that after the wallpaper was changed, it would be the heavy bedstead. And then the barred windows. And then the gate at the head of the stairs, and so on.

"You know the place is doing you good," he said. "And really, dear, I don't care to redo the house. Not just for a three-month rental."

"Then do let us go downstairs," I said. "There are such pretty rooms there."

Then he took me in his arms and called me a blessed little goose. He said he would go down to the cellar, if I wished. And he would have it painted white.

But he is right enough about the beds and windows and things.

It is as airy and comfortable a room as anyone might wish. Of course, I would not be so silly as to make him uncomfortable just for a **whim.**

I'm really getting quite fond of the big room, all but that horrid paper.

Out of one window, I can see the garden. There are mysterious, deep-shaded arbors, unruly, old-fashioned flowers, and bushes and twisted trees.

Out of another window, I get a lovely view of the bay. And I can see a little private wharf⁴ belonging to the estate. There is a beautiful shaded lane that runs down there from the house. I always imagine I see people walking in these many paths and arbors.

But John has warned me not to give way to daydreams in the least. He says not to use my imaginative power and habit of making up stories. With such things, a nervous weakness like mine is sure to lead to all kinds of excited **fantasies.** He says that I ought to use my will and good sense to stop doing that. So I try.

I wish sometimes that I were well enough to write a little. I think it would relieve the press of ideas and rest me.

But I find I get rather tired when I try.

It is so discouraging not to have any friends to talk with me about my work. When I get really well, John says we will ask Cousin Henry and Julia down for a long visit. But he would not let me have such interesting people about now. He says he would just as soon put fireworks in my pillowcase.

I wish I could be well faster.

But I must not think about that. This paper looks to me as if it *knows* what a cruel **influence** it has!

There is a repeating spot where the pattern droops like a broken neck. Two bulging eyes stare at you upside down.

⁴A wharf is a wooden platform at water's edge used for docking boats.

I get really angry with the boldness of it. And it goes on forever. Up and down and sideways the patterns crawl. And those **absurd** unblinking eyes are everywhere. There is one place where two pieces don't match up. The eyes go all up and down the line, one a little higher than the other.

I never saw so much expression in a lifeless thing before. And we all know how much expression lifeless things can have! I used to lie awake as a child. I got more entertainment and terror out of blank walls and plain furniture than most children could find in a toy store.

I remember what a kindly wink the knobs of our big, old cabinet used to have. And there was one chair that always seemed like a strong friend.

I felt that I didn't have to worry about any of the other things looking too fierce. I could always hop into that chair and be safe.

The furniture in this room is no worse than mismatched, however. We had to bring it all from downstairs. I suppose when this was used as a playroom, they had to take the nursery things out. And no wonder! I never saw such destruction as the children have made here.

The wallpaper, as I said before, is torn off in spots. And it sticks closer than a brother. They must have been determined as well as full of hatred.

The floor is scratched and gouged and splintered. The plaster itself is dug out here and there. This great, heavy bed is all we found in the room. It looks as if it had been through the wars.

But I don't mind it a bit—only the paper.

Here comes John's sister. Such a dear girl she is, and so careful of me! I must not let her find me writing.

She is a perfect and cheerful housekeeper, and she hopes for no better work. I truly believe she thinks it is the writing that made me sick!

But I can write when she is out. And luckily, I can see her a long way off from these windows.

There is one window that looks over the road. It is a

lovely, shaded winding road. And one window just looks off over the country. A lovely country too, full of great elms and soft meadows.

The wallpaper has a kind of under-pattern in a different shade. It is very irritating. You can only see it in certain lights, and not clearly then.

But in some places, the paper isn't faded. There—when the sun is just so—I can see a strange, stirring, formless sort of figure. It seems to sneak about behind that silly and glaring front design.

There's sister on the stairs!

Well, the Fourth of July is over! The people are all gone, and I am tired out. John thought it might do me good to see a little company. So we just had Mother and Nellie and the children down for a week.

I didn't do a thing, of course. Jennie sees to everything now.

But it tired me all the same.

John says that if I don't pick up faster, he shall send me to Weir Mitchell[5] in the fall.

But I don't want to go there at all. I had a friend who was in his hands once. She says he is just like John and my brother, only more so!

Besides, it would be such a chore to go so far.

I don't feel as if it is worthwhile to do anything. I'm getting dreadfully worried and fussy. I cry at nothing, and cry most of the time. Of course I don't when John is here, or anybody else. Only when I am alone. And I am alone a good deal just now. John is kept in town very often by serious cases. Jennie is good and lets me alone when I want her to.

So I walk a little in the garden or down that lovely lane. I sit on the porch under the roses. And I lie down up here a good deal.

I'm getting really fond of the room despite the wallpaper. Perhaps *because* of the wallpaper.

It stays on my mind so!

[5] S. Weir Mitchell (1829–1914) was an author and physician who specialized in treating women.

I lie here on this great immovable bed—it is nailed down, I believe. I follow that pattern about by the hour. It is as good as exercise, I assure you.

I start, we'll say, at the bottom. Down in the corner over there where it has not been touched. I make a decision for the thousandth time. I *will* follow that pointless pattern to some sort of an end.

I know a little of the **principle** of design. So I know this thing was not arranged on any laws I ever heard of. The pattern does not spread out from the center or switch back and forth or repeat. Nor does it have **symmetry.**

It is repeated, of course, on each sheet of paper, but not otherwise. Looked at in one way, each sheet stands alone. The bloated curves and flourishes go waddling up and down in separate columns of foolishness. They look like they are in *delirium tremens.*[6]

But, on the other hand, they connect diagonally. The outlines run off in great slanting waves of visual horror. They are like a lot of rolling seaweed chasing one another.

The whole thing goes horizontally too. At least it seems so. I exhaust myself trying to see the pattern going in that direction.

They have used a horizontal sheet for a frieze.[7] That adds wonderfully to the confusion.

There is one end of the room where the paper is almost undamaged. When the cross light fades, the low sun shines directly upon it, and I can almost imagine something spreading out in the middle. The endless weird images seem to form around a common center. Then they rush off in headlong plunges of equal confusion.

It makes me tired to follow it, so I will take a nap.

I don't know why I should write this.

I don't want to.

I don't feel able.

And I know John would think it absurd. But I *must* say what I feel and think in some way. It is such a relief!

But the effort is getting to be greater than the relief.

[6]*Delirium tremens* is Latin for "state of mental confusion."
[7]A frieze is a decorative horizontal band on the upper part of a wall.

Half the time now I am awfully lazy and lie down ever so much.

John says I mustn't lose my strength. He gives me cod liver oil and lots of tonics and things—to say nothing of ale and wine and rare meat.

Dear John! He loves me very dearly and hates to have me sick. I tried to have an earnest, **reasonable** talk with him the other day. I wanted to tell him how I wish he would let me go. I want to visit Cousin Henry and Julia.

But he said I wasn't able to go. Nor would I be able to stand it after I got there. I did not make out a very good case for myself. I was crying before I had finished.

It is getting to be a great effort for me to think straight. Just this nervous weakness, I suppose.

Dear John gathered me up in his arms, carried me upstairs, and laid me on the bed. He sat by me and read to me until I tired.

He said I was his darling and his comfort and all he had. And that I must take care of myself and keep well for his sake.

He says that I must help myself. I must use my will and self-control and not let any silly imagination run away with me.

There's one comfort—the baby is well and happy. I am glad that he does not have to live in this nursery with the horrid wallpaper.

If we had not used it, that blessed child would have! Why, I wouldn't have a child of mine live in such a room for anything. He is such a sensitive little thing.

I never thought of it before, but it is lucky that John kept me here after all. I can stand it so much easier than a baby can, you see.

Of course, I never mention the wallpaper to them anymore. I am too wise. But I keep watching it all the same.

There are things in that paper that nobody but I will ever know.

Behind that outside pattern, the dim shapes get clearer every day.

It is always the same shape, but many of them.

And it is like a woman stooping down and creeping about behind that pattern. I don't like it a bit. I wonder—I begin to think—I wish John would take me away from here!

It is so hard to talk with John about my case. That is because he is so wise, and because he loves me so.

But I tried it last night.

It was moonlight. The moon shines in all around, just as the sun does.

I hate to see it sometimes, it creeps so slowly. The moonlight always comes in by one window or another.

John was asleep, and I hated to waken him. So I kept still. I watched the moonlight on that bulging wallpaper until I felt creepy.

The faint figure behind seemed to shake the pattern. It looked just as if she wanted to get out.

I got up softly and went to see if the paper *did* move. When I came back, John was awake.

"What is it, little girl?" he asked gently. "Don't go walking about like that—you'll get cold."

I thought it was a good time to talk. So I told him that I really was not gaining ground here. I said that I wished he would take me away.

"Why, darling!" he said. "Our lease will be up in three weeks. I can't see how to leave before.

"The repairs are not done at home," he went on. "And I cannot possibly leave town just now. Naturally, if you were in any danger, I could and would. But you really are better, dear, whether you can see it or not. I am a doctor, dear, and I know. You are gaining flesh and color. Your appetite is better. I feel much better about you."

"I don't weigh a bit more," I said. "Nor as much as I did before. And my appetite may be better in the evening when you are here. But it is worse in the morning when you are away!"

"Bless her little heart!" said he with a big hug. "She shall be as sick as she pleases! But now let's improve the shining hours by going to sleep. We'll talk about it in the morning."

"And you won't go away?" I asked gloomily.

"Why, how can I, dear? It is only three weeks more. Then we will take a nice little trip of a few days while Jennie is getting the house ready. Really, dear, you are better!"

"Better in body perhaps—" I began. I stopped short because he sat up straight and looked at me with a stern, accusing look. I could not say another word.

"My darling," he said. "I beg of you, for my sake and for our child's sake, as well as for your own. You must never for one instant let that idea enter your mind! There is nothing as dangerous or as fascinating to a nature like yours. It is a false and foolish idea. Can you not trust me as a physician when I tell you so?"

So, of course, I said no more about it. We went to sleep before long. He thought I was asleep first, but I wasn't. I lay there for hours staring at that front pattern and then the back pattern. I was trying to decide whether they really did move together or separately.

On a pattern like this, by daylight, there is a lack of order. It makes so little sense that it constantly bothers a normal mind.

The color is horrible enough and unreliable enough and maddening enough. But the pattern is a torture.

You think you have mastered it. But just as you get well underway in following, it turns a somersault. And there you are. It slaps you in the face, knocks you down, and tramples upon you. It is like a bad dream.

The outside pattern is a flowery design. It reminds one of a fungus. If you can, imagine a toadstool in pieces—an endless string of toadstools. Imagine them budding and sprouting in endless coils. Why, that is something like it.

That is, sometimes!

There is one thing unusually strange about this paper. It is a thing nobody seems to notice but myself. That is that it changes as the light changes.

I always watch for the first long, straight ray of sun shooting in through the east window. Then the paper changes so quickly that I can never quite believe it.

That is why I watch it always.

The moon shines in all night when there is a moon. By the moonlight, I wouldn't know it was the same paper.

At night, in any kind of light, it becomes changed. In twilight, candlelight, lamplight, and worst of all by moonlight, it becomes bars. The outside pattern I mean. And the woman behind it is as plain as can be.

I didn't realize for a long time what that dim underpattern was. The thing shows through from behind. But now I am quite sure it is a woman.

By daylight she is subdued, quiet. I imagine it is the pattern that keeps her so still. It is so puzzling. It keeps me quiet by the hour.

I lie down ever so much now. John says it is good for me and to sleep all I can.

Indeed, he started the habit. He made me lie down for an hour after each meal.

It is a very bad habit, I am convinced. For you see, I don't sleep.

And that causes me to lie. For I don't tell them I'm awake—oh, no!

I hate to say it, but I am getting a little afraid of John.

He seems very queer sometimes. Even Jennie has an odd look.

It strikes me occasionally—that perhaps it is the paper!

I have watched John when he did not know I was looking. And I have come into the room suddenly on the most innocent of excuses. I've caught him several times *looking at the paper.* And Jennie too. I caught Jennie with her hand on it once.

She didn't know I was in the room. I spoke in the most polite manner possible. I asked her in a very quiet voice what she was doing with the paper. She turned around as if she had been caught stealing. She looked quite angry. She asked me why I should frighten her so!

Then she said that the paper stained everything it touched. She had found yellow stains on all my clothes and John's. She said she wished we would be more careful!

Did not that sound innocent? But I know she was studying that pattern. And I am determined that nobody shall find it out but myself!

Life is very much more exciting now than it used to be. You see, I have something more to expect. I have something to look forward to, to watch. I really do eat better and am more quiet than I was.

John is so pleased to see me improve! He laughed a little the other day. He said I seemed to be doing well in spite of my wallpaper.

I turned it off with a laugh. I certainly wasn't going to tell him it was *because* of the wallpaper. He would make fun of me. He might even want to take me away.

I don't want to leave now until I have found it out. There is one more week. I think that will be enough.

I'm feeling ever so much better! I don't sleep much at night, for it is so interesting to watch developments. But I sleep a good deal in the daytime.

In the daytime, it is boring and puzzling.

There are always new shoots on the fungus. There are new shades of yellow all over it. I cannot keep count of them, though I have tried very hard.

It is the strangest yellow, that wallpaper! It makes me think of all the yellow things I ever saw. Not beautiful things, like buttercups, but old, foul, bad yellow things.

But there is something else about that paper—the smell! I noticed it the moment we came into the room.

But with so much air and sun, it was not bad. Now we have had a week of fog and rain. Whether the windows are open or not, the smell is here.

It creeps all over the house.

I find it floating in the dining room and sneaking into the parlor. I find it hiding in the hall and lying in wait for me on the stairs.

It gets into my hair.

Even when I go to ride, if I turn my head suddenly and surprise it—there is that smell!

Such a peculiar odor it is! I have spent hours trying to study it, to find what it smelled like.

It is not bad—at first. It is very gentle and quite faint. But it is the longest-lasting odor I ever met.

It is awful in this damp weather. I wake up in the night and find it hanging over me.

It used to disturb me at first. I thought seriously of burning the house—to reach the smell.

But now I am used to it. The only thing I can think of that it is like is the *color* of the paper. A yellow smell!

There is a very funny mark on this wall. It is low down, near the baseboard. A streak that runs round the room. It goes behind every piece of furniture except the bed. It is a long, straight, even scar, as if it had been rubbed over and over.

I wonder how it was done and who did it. And what they did it for. Round and round and round—round and round and round—it makes me dizzy!

I really have discovered something at last.

Through watching so much at night, when it changes so, I have finally found out.

The front pattern does move—and no wonder! The woman behind shakes it.

Sometimes I think there are a great many women behind. Sometimes only one. She crawls about quickly, and her crawling shakes it all over.

In the very bright spots, she keeps still. Then, in the very shady spots, she just takes hold of the bars. She shakes them hard.

And she is trying to climb through all the time. But nobody could climb through that pattern—it strangles so. I think that is why it has so many heads.

They get through, and then the pattern chokes them off. It turns them upside down and makes their eyes white!

If those heads were covered or taken off, it would not be half as bad.

I think that woman gets out in the daytime! And I'll tell you why—privately. I've seen her! I can see her out of every one of my windows!

It is the same woman, I know, for she is always creeping. Most women do not creep by daylight.

I see her on that long road under the trees, creeping along. When a carriage comes she hides under the blackberry vines.

I don't blame her a bit. It must be very **humiliating** to be caught creeping by daylight!

I always lock the door when I creep by daylight. I can't do it at night. I know John would suspect something at once.

And John is so odd now that I don't want to irritate him. I wish he would take another room! Besides, I don't want anybody to get that woman out at night.

I often wonder if I could see her out of all the windows at once.

But, turn as fast as I can, I can only see out of one window at a time.

And I always see her. But she *may* be able to creep faster than I can turn.

I have watched her sometimes away off in the open country. She creeps as fast as a cloud shadow in a high wind.

*   *   *

If only that top pattern could be gotten off the one underneath! I mean to try it, little by little.

I have found out another funny thing, but I shan't tell it this time! It does not do to trust people too much.

There are only two more days to get this paper off. I believe John is beginning to notice. I don't like the look in his eyes. And I heard him ask Jennie a lot of medical questions about me. She had a very good report to give.

She said I slept a good deal in the daytime.

Even though I'm so quiet, John knows I don't sleep very well at night!

He asked me all sorts of questions too. He pretended to be very loving and kind—as if I couldn't see through him!

Still, it's no wonder he acts so. He has been sleeping under this paper for three months.

It interests only me. But I feel sure John and Jennie are secretly affected by it.

Hurrah! This is the last day, but it is enough. John is to stay in town overnight. He won't be out here until this evening.

Jennie wanted to sleep in the room with me—the sly thing! But I told her I would surely rest better for a night all alone.

That was clever, for really I wasn't alone at all! As soon as it was moonlight, that poor thing began to crawl and shake the pattern. I got up and ran to help her.

I pulled, and she shook. I shook, and she pulled. Before morning, the two of us had peeled off yards and yards of that paper.

A strip about as high as my head and halfway around the room.

And then the sun came—and that awful pattern began to laugh at me! I declared I would finish it today!

Jennie looked at the wall in amazement. But I told her merrily that I did it out of pure spite at the vicious thing.

She laughed and said she wouldn't mind doing it herself. Then she warned me against getting tired.

How she betrayed herself that time!

But I am here. No person touches this paper but me—not *alive!*

She tried to get me out of the room—it was too obvious! But I said it was quiet and empty and clean now. I believed I would lie down again and sleep all I could. I said not to wake me, not even for dinner—I would call when I woke.

So now she is gone. The servants are gone, and the things are gone. There is nothing left in the room but that nailed-down bed with the canvas mattress we found on it.

We shall sleep downstairs tonight and take the boat home tomorrow.

Now that it is bare again, I quite enjoy the room.

How those children did tear about here!

This bed frame is clearly gnawed!

But I must get to work.

I have locked the door and thrown the key down into the front path.

I don't want to go out. And I don't want to have anybody come in until John comes.

I want to surprise him.

I've got a rope up here that even Jennie did not find. If that woman does get out and tries to get away, I can tie her.

But I forgot I could not reach far without anything to stand on!

This bed will *not* move!

I tried to lift and push it until I was lame. Then I got so angry that I bit off a little piece at one corner—but it hurt my teeth.

Then I peeled off all the paper I could reach standing on the floor. It sticks horribly, and the pattern just enjoys it! All those strangled heads and bulging eyes and waddling fungus growths—they just shriek with laughter!

I am getting angry enough to do something desperate. To jump out the window would be fine exercise. But the bars are too strong for me to even try.

Besides, I wouldn't do it. Of course not. I know well enough that a step like that is improper. It might be misunderstood.

I don't even like to look out of the windows anymore. There are so many of those creeping women, and they creep so fast.

I wonder if they all came out of that wallpaper as I did?

But I am securely fastened now by my well-hidden rope. You don't get *me* out in the road there.

I suppose I shall have to get back behind the pattern when night comes. That is hard!

It is so pleasant to be out in this great room and creep around as I please!

I don't want to go outside. I won't, even if Jennie asks me to.

For outside you have to creep on the ground, and everything is green instead of yellow.

But here I can creep smoothly on the floor. My shoulder just fits in that long scar around the wall. So I cannot lose my way.

Why, there's John at the door!

It's no use, young man. You can't open it!

How he does call and pound!

Now he's crying for an ax.

It would be a shame to break down that beautiful door!

"John, dear!" said I in the gentlest voice. "The key is down by the front steps. It is under a plantain leaf!"

And then I said it several more times. I spoke very gently and slowly. I said it so often that he had to go and see. He got it, of course, and came in. He stopped short by the door.

"What is the matter?" he cried. "For God's sake, what are you doing?"

124

I kept on creeping just the same. But I looked at him over my shoulder.

"I've got out at last," I said. "In spite of you and Jennie. And I've pulled off most of the paper so you can't put me back!"

Now why should that man have fainted? But he did, and right across my path next to the wall. I had to creep over him every time!

INSIGHTS INTO CHARLOTTE PERKINS GILMAN (1860–1935)

"The Yellow Wallpaper" is more than a horror story. It's also an accurate account of how women were regarded fewer than one hundred years ago. A woman was expected to be a homemaker and to cultivate few interests or skills beyond the care of her family. It was widely assumed that women were mentally and emotionally inferior to men. Charlotte Perkins Gilman knew from personal experience the damaging effects of this kind of stereotyping.

Gilman was born in Hartford, Connecticut. As a child, she watched the painful breakup of her family. Her own first marriage ended in divorce, as well. Gilman also suffered from severe clinical depression. Despite all this, she devoted her time and energy to women's issues. She wrote books, articles, and stories and lectured about the prejudice and discrimination faced by women.

The doctor who treated Gilman's depression was named S. Weir Mitchell, the same doctor the narrator in the story refuses to see. Mitchell was a famous writer and doctor who specialized in women's medical and mental problems. His prescription for Gilman was to stay at home. In addition, she was to work and think as little as possible. Above all else, she was not to do the reading or writing that was so important to her. It is now generally thought that Mitchell did most of his patients more harm than good.

Gilman kept working and lecturing until her death in 1935.

Other works by Charlotte Perkins Gilman:
The Living of Charlotte Perkins Gilman, autobiography
Moving the Mountain, novel
Women and Economics, nonfiction

THE SIGNALMAN

CHARLES DICKENS

VOCABULARY PREVIEW

Below is a list of words that appear in the story. Read the list and get to know the words before you start the story.

calamity—disaster; accident
circumstances—situation; course of events
clammy—damp; moist
descent—downward climb
desperate—beyond hope; extreme
disloyal—deceiving; double-crossing
dismal—cheerless; gloomy
earnestly—eagerly
expectation—hopefulness
forbidding—unfriendly; threatening
hoarse—rough; cracked
idle—unimportant; purposeless
involuntarily—automatically; without thinking
manual—requiring human physical skill and energy
post—assigned spot or location; station
routine—habit; daily pattern
signal—sign; warning
supernatural—magical; mysterious
telegraphed—sent a message by wire
yonder—at a distance; afar

The Signalman

In the early days of the railroad, a signalman guided trains safely past dangerous areas. The signalman worked alone in a small, box-like structure hour after hour. There was a lot of time to daydream and imagine things.

"Hello! Below there!"

When he heard a voice calling to him, he was standing at the door of his box. In his hands, he held a flag that was rolled around its short pole. One would have thought he would know where the voice came from.

I stood on the top of the steep hollow that was nearly over his head. But instead of looking up, he turned himself about and looked down the Line.[1] There was something strange in the way he did so, but for the life of me, I could not decide what it was.

His figure looked shortened and shadowed down in the trench. And mine was high above him. I was soaked in the glow of an angry sunset. I had to shade my eyes to see him at all.

"Hello! Below!"

[1]The Line refers to a section of the track.

He turned himself around again from looking down the Line. Raising his eyes, he saw my figure high above him.

"Is there any path by which I can come down and speak to you?"

He looked up at me without replying. I did not push him too soon by repeating my **idle** question. Just then came a vague shaking in the earth and air. It quickly changed to a violent throb. Then it became an oncoming rush that caused me to jump back. It felt like it had enough power to pull me down.

Steam rose to my height from this rapid train. It passed me and went racing over the landscape. As I looked down again, I saw him rolling up the flag he had shown while the train went by.

I repeated my call. He paused and stared at me. Then he motioned with his rolled-up flag toward a point on my level. It was some two or three hundred yards away.

I called down to him, "All right!"

I headed toward that point and looked carefully around. I found a rough zigzag path carved out. I followed it into the hollow.

The hollow was very deep and unusually steep. It cut through a **clammy** stone that became oozier and wetter as I went down. For these reasons, I found the trip long. It gave me time to recall something strange about his attitude—he had looked unwilling to point out the path.

When I came down low enough on the zigzag **descent,** I could see him again. He was standing between the rails of the track on which the train had just passed. He looked as if he was waiting for me to appear.

He had his left hand at his chin. That left elbow rested on his right hand, which was crossed over his chest. His attitude was one of **expectation** and watchfulness. I stopped for a moment and wondered about it.

I resumed my downward path. Stepping upon the level of the railroad, I drew near him. I saw that he was a very pale man; he seemed almost lifeless. He had a dark beard and rather heavy eyebrows.

His **post** was in as lonely and **dismal** a place as I had ever seen. On either side was a dripping wet wall of jagged stone. The view to one side was just a crooked addition to this great pit. The shorter view was in the other direction. It ended in a gloomy red danger light that warned trains of the approaching tunnel. Next to it was an even gloomier entrance to a black tunnel. The huge tunnel had a **forbidding** look.

Very little sunlight ever found its way to this spot. It had an earthy, deadly smell. A great deal of cold wind rushed through it. It chilled me, and I felt as if I had left the natural world for a moment.

Before he stirred, I was near enough to touch him. Even then, he did not remove his eyes from mine. He took one step back and lifted his hand.

This was a lonesome post to have, I said. It had caught my attention when I looked down from up **yonder.** A visitor was rare, I should suppose—and I hoped I wasn't unwelcome. I told him that I had been shut up within narrow limits all of my life. Since I had been at last set free, I had a newly awakened interest in seeing how things work.

I know that I spoke to him of these things, but I am far from sure of the words I used. I am not happy starting any conversation. And there was something about the man that disturbed me.

He directed a curious look toward the red light near the tunnel's mouth. He looked all around it—for what, I do not know—and then he looked at me.

"That light is part of your job, is it not?" I asked.

He answered in a low voice, "Don't you know it is?"

A horrible thought came to me as I studied his fixed eyes and gloomy face. I thought that this was a ghost, not a man. And I have wondered ever since whether there may have been an illness in his mind.

At this thought, I stepped back. Then I saw a flash of fear in his eyes. This put my horrible thought into flight.

I forced a smile. "You look at me," I said, "as if you were afraid of me."

"I was wondering," he answered, "whether I had seen you before."

"Where?"

He pointed to the red light.

"There?" I asked.

Carefully watching me, he replied (but without sound), "Yes."

"My good fellow, what would I do there? I never was—you may swear to it."

"Yes, I am sure I may," he replied.

His attitude cleared, as did my own. He now replied to my remarks with ease and eloquence.

Had he much to do here?

Yes. That was to say, he had enough responsibility to bear. Care and watchfulness were required of him. Of actual **manual** labor, he had next to none. He had to change that **signal**, to adjust those lights. He had to turn this iron handle now and then. That was all he had to do of that kind.

He thought I seemed to make too much of those long and lonely hours. He could only say that the **routine** of his life had shaped itself into that form. He had grown used to it.

He had taught himself a foreign language down here—that is, if knowing it only by sight could be considered learning it. (He had formed his own crude ideas of its sound.) He had also worked at mastering fractions and decimals. He had tried a little algebra. But he was, he said, a poor hand at figures.

Was it necessary for him when on duty to remain in that hollow? Must he stay in that damp air? Could he never rise into the sunshine from between those high stone walls?

Well, that depended upon **circumstances.** Under some conditions, there was less traffic on the Line than under others. The same held true for certain hours of the day and night.

In good weather, he tried to find time to rise above these depths. But he was always likely to be called by his electric bell. At such times, he had to listen for it with double concern. So the relief was less than I would suppose.

He took me into his box. There was a fire there. There was a desk for an official book in which he had to make certain entries. There was a telegraph. And there was the little bell he had spoken of.

I trusted that he would excuse my saying that he had been well educated. I added that he was perhaps educated above this position. (I hoped I said this without insulting him.)

He said that such occurrences were not rare, that they were often found in large groups of men. He said he had heard it was so in workhouses,[2] the police force, and even in that last **desperate** resort, the army. And he *knew* it was so in any great railway staff.

He said that he had once been a student of natural science. He had attended lectures. But he had run wild and misused his chances. He had slid down and never risen again. He had no complaint to offer about it. He had made his choices and was willing to live with the consequences.

He said all of this in a quiet manner. His serious, dark glances were divided between the fire and me. He threw in the word *sir* from time to time, especially when he talked about his youth. He wanted me to understand that he claimed to be nothing but what I could see.

He was interrupted several times by the little bell. Then he had to read off messages and send replies. Or he had to stand outside the door and display a flag as a train passed.

He exchanged some words with the driver. In carrying out his duties, he was exact and alert. Several times he broke off his talk abruptly and remained silent until he had done what was needed.

[2]During Dickens' time, the poor were often forced to live and work in miserable places known as workhouses.

I should have considered this man one of the safest to hold that job. However, twice while speaking to me, he stopped and became pale. He turned toward the little bell when it did *not* ring. He opened the door of the hut. He looked out toward the red light near the mouth of the tunnel. Both times he came back to the fire with a look I could not explain. It was the same look I had noticed when we were so far apart, and I had not been able to define it.

When I rose to leave him, I said, "You almost make me think that I have met with a contented man."

(I must admit that I said this to lead him on.)

"I believe I used to be," he replied in the low voice in which he had first spoken. "But I am troubled, sir, I am troubled."

I could tell that he would have taken back the words if he could. But he had said them, and I took them up quickly.

"What are you troubled by?"

"It is very difficult to explain, sir. It is very, very difficult to speak of. But if you ever visit me again, I will try to tell you."

"But I definitely intend to visit again. When shall it be?"

"I shall be on again at ten tomorrow night, sir."

"I will come at eleven."

He thanked me and went out the door with me.

"I'll show my white light, sir," he said in his strange low voice, "until you have found the way up. When you have found it, don't call out! And when you are at the top, don't call out!"

His manner made the place feel colder. But I simply said, "Very well."

"And when you come down tomorrow night, don't call out! Let me ask you a parting question. What made you cry, 'Hello! Below there!' tonight?"

"Heaven knows," I said. "I cried something like that—"

"Not like that, sir. Those were the very words. I know them well."

"I said them, no doubt, because I saw you below."

"For no other reason?"

"What other reason could I possibly have?"

"You have no feeling that they were given to you in any **supernatural** way?"

"No."

He wished me good-night and held up his light. I walked by the side of the rails until I found the path. (I had a very unpleasant feeling that a train was coming behind me.) It was easier to climb than to descend. So I got back to my inn without any adventures.

I was on time for my meeting the next night. I placed my foot on the first step of the zigzag path as the distant clocks were striking eleven. He was waiting for me at the bottom with his white light on.

"I have not called out," I said, when we were close together. "May I speak now?"

"Of course, sir."

"Good evening, then, and here's my hand."

"Good evening, sir, and here's mine."

With that, we walked side by side to his box. We entered it, closed the door, and sat down by the fire.

"I have made up my mind, sir," he began. He was bending forward and speaking only a little above a whisper. "You shall not have to ask me twice what troubles me. I took you for someone else yesterday evening. That troubles me."

"That mistake?"

"No. That someone else."

"Who is it?"

"I don't know."

"Like me?"

"I don't know. I never saw the face. The left arm is across the face, and the right arm is waved. Violently waved. This way."

I followed his action with my eyes. It was the action of an arm gesturing with the greatest passion and force. It made me think of the words *"For God's sake, clear the way!"*

"One moonlit night," said the man, "I was sitting here. I heard a voice cry, 'Hello! Below there!' I jumped up and looked from that door. I saw him standing by the red light near the tunnel. He was waving as I just showed you. The voice seemed **hoarse** with shouting. It cried, 'Look out! Look out!' And then again, 'Hello! Below there!'

"I caught up my lamp and turned it on red. I ran toward the figure calling, 'What's wrong? What has happened? Where?' It stood just outside the blackness of the tunnel. I came so close to it that I had my hand stretched out to pull the sleeve away. Then it was gone."

"Into the tunnel?" I asked.

"No. I ran on into the tunnel, five hundred yards. I stopped and held my lamp above my head. I saw the figures of the measured distance. I saw the wet stains stealing down the walls and trickling through the arch. I ran out again, faster than I had run in. A mortal terror of the place had come over me.

"I looked all around the red light with my own red light. I went up the iron ladder to the gallery[3] on top of the tunnel. And I came down again and ran back here. I **telegraphed** both ways— 'An alarm has been given. Is anything wrong?' The answer came back, both ways— 'All is well.' "

I resisted the slow touch of a frozen finger tracing my spine. I explained to him how this figure must have been a trick of his sense of sight.

I told him about diseases of the delicate nerves that work the eye. Such figures were known to have troubled many patients.

"As to an imaginary cry," I said, "listen for a moment to the wind in this unnatural valley. Do you hear the wild harp music it makes of the telegraph wires?"

[3]A gallery is a balcony.

We sat listening for a while. That was all very well, he replied, but he ought to know something of the wind and the wires. He had often passed long winter nights here, alone and watching. Then he begged to say that he had not finished.

I asked his pardon.

Touching my arm, he slowly added these words, "Within six hours after the Appearance, the famous accident on this Line happened. Within ten hours, the dead and wounded were brought through the tunnel. They were carried over the spot where the figure had stood."

A disagreeable shudder crept over me, but I did my best to fight it. It could not be denied, I replied, that this was a remarkable coincidence. It was certain to affect him deeply. But it was true that remarkable coincidences happen constantly. And that they must be taken into account in dealing with such a subject. (To be sure, I added, men of common sense did not allow much for coincidences. Not in making life's ordinary plans.)

He again begged to say that he had not finished.

I again begged his pardon for having interrupted again.

"This was just a year ago," he said, placing his hand upon my arm. He glanced over his shoulder with hollow eyes. "Six or seven months passed, and I had recovered from the surprise and shock. Then I was standing at the door one morning. It was daybreak. I looked toward the red light and saw the ghost again."

"Did it cry out?"

"No. It was silent."

"Did it wave its arm?"

"No. It leaned against the shaft of the light with both hands before its face. Like this."

Once more, I followed his action with my eyes. It was an action of mourning. I have seen such a pose in stone figures on tombs.

"Did you go up to it?"

"I came in and sat down, partly to collect my thoughts. It had made me feel faint. When I went to the door again, daylight was above me. And the ghost was gone."

"But nothing followed? Nothing came of this?"

He touched me on the arm with his forefinger three times. He gave a fearful nod each time.

"Something happened that very day. As a train came out of the tunnel, I noticed something at a carriage window on my side. It looked like a confusion of hands and heads, and something waved. I saw it just in time to signal the driver—Stop!

"He shut off and put his brake on. But the train drifted past here 150 yards or more. I ran after it, and I heard terrible screams and cries. A beautiful young woman had died instantly in one of the rooms. She was brought in here and laid down on this floor between us."

I pushed my chair back **involuntarily.** I looked at the floor and then at him.

"True, sir. True. I tell it to you exactly as it happened."

I could think of nothing to say that might help. My mouth was very dry. The wind and the wires took up the story with a long, sorrowful wail.

He went on. "Now, sir, mark this and judge how my mind is troubled. The ghost came back a week ago. Ever since, it has been there now and again, by fits and starts."

"At the light?"

"At the Danger light."

"What does it seem to do?"

With great passion, he repeated that earlier gesture that made me think of *"For God's sake clear the way!"*

Then he went on. "I have no peace or rest from it. It calls to me in a tortured manner for many minutes at a time— 'Below there! Look out! Look out!' It stands waving to me. It rings my little bell—"

I stopped him at that. "Did it ring your bell yesterday evening when I was here? When you went to the door?"

"Twice."

"Why, see how your imagination misleads you?" I reasoned. "My eyes were on the bell, and my ears were open to the bell. And if I am a living man, it did *not* ring at those times. Nor at any other time. Not except when it was rung in the natural course of your everyday work. That was the station communicating with you."

He shook his head. "I have never made a mistake about that, sir. I have never confused the ghost's ring with the man's. The ghost's ring is a strange vibration in the bell. It gets that sound from nothing else. And I have not said that the bell's vibration can be seen. I don't wonder that you failed to hear it. But *I* heard it."

"And did the ghost seem to be there when you looked out?"

"It *was* there."

"Both times?"

He repeated firmly, "Both times."

"Will you come to the door with me and look for it now?"

He bit his lower lip. He seemed somewhat unwilling, but he arose. I opened the door and stood on the step while he stood in the doorway. There was the Danger light. There was the dismal mouth of the tunnel. There were the high stone walls of the hollow. There were the stars above them.

"Do you see it?" I asked, taking careful note of his face. His eyes were big and strained—indeed, my own eyes had grown very large when I looked **earnestly** toward the same spot.

"No," he answered. "It is not there."

"Agreed," I said.

We went in again, shut the door, and took our seats. I was thinking how best to improve on this progress, if it might be called that. Then he took up the conversation in a natural way. He seemed to assume that there could be no serious question of fact between us. I felt myself in the weakest of positions.

"By this time, you will fully understand, sir," he said.

"What troubles me so dreadfully is the question—what does the ghost mean?"

I was *not* sure, I told him, that I fully understood.

"What is it warning against?" he asked, thinking it over. His eyes were on the fire.

"What is the danger? Where is the danger? There is danger hanging over us somewhere on the Line. Some dreadful **calamity** will happen. It is not to be doubted a third time. Not after what has already happened. But surely this is a cruel haunting of *me*. What can *I* do!"

He pulled out his handkerchief and wiped the drops from his heated forehead.

"I can telegraph to either side of me, or both. But if I telegraph 'Danger,' I can give no reason for it."

He went on, wiping the palms of his hands. "I would get into trouble and do no good. They would think I was mad. This is the way it would work—Message: 'Danger! Take care!' Answer: 'What Danger? Where?' Message: 'Don't know. But for God's sake, take care!' They would replace me. What else could they do?"

His pain of mind was most pitiful to see. It was the mental torture of a responsible man given more than he could bear. He was weighed down by a responsibility that was impossible to figure out.

"When it first stood under the Danger light, why did it not tell me?" he went on. He pushed his dark hair back from his face. He drew his hands across his temples in feverish worry.

"Why didn't it tell me where the accident was to happen? Why didn't it tell me *how* it could be avoided? On its second coming, it hid its face. Why not tell me instead— 'She is going to die. Let them keep her at home'?

"Perhaps it came on those two occasions only to show me that its warnings were true. If it wanted to prepare me for the third, why not warn me plainly now? And I, Lord help me! A mere signalman on this lonely station! Why not go to somebody higher up, somebody with the power to act?"

When I saw him in this state, I saw what I had to do for the present. For the poor man's sake, as well as for the public's safety, I had to calm his mind. Therefore, I put aside all question of reality or unreality that stood between us.

I told him that he must carry on with his duties. And that it should comfort him that he understood his duties. Even though he did not understand these confusing appearances. I succeeded in this effort far better than in the attempt to reason him out of his beliefs. He became calm.

As the night went on, the duties connected with his job began to make larger demands on his attention. I left him at two in the morning. I had offered to stay through the night, but he would not hear of it.

I looked back at the red light more than once as I went up the pathway. I did not like the red light. I would have slept poorly if my bed had been under it. I see no reason to conceal any of this. Nor did I like the two events of the accident and the dead girl. I see no reason to conceal that, either.

But what ran most in my thoughts was the question— How should I act? Something had been revealed to me. I had proved the man to be intelligent, watchful, careful, and exact. But in his state of mind, how long might he remain so?

Though in a low position, he held a most important trust. Would I (for instance) like to stake my own life on him? What were the chances that he would continue to do his job well?

I was unable to overcome a feeling that there would be something **disloyal** in my telling what he had told me. I could not speak to his superiors in the company. First, I must be plain with him and propose a middle course.

I finally decided to offer to go with him to the wisest medical doctor we could find in those parts. We would get the doctor's opinion. (Otherwise, I would keep his secret for the present.)

He told me that a change in his work schedule would come around the next night. He would be off an hour or two after sunrise and on again soon after sunset. I made plans to return after sunset.

The next evening was a lovely evening. I walked out early to enjoy it. The sun was not quite down when I crossed the path near the top of the deep hollow. I would extend my walk for an hour, I said to myself. It would then be time to go to my signalman's box.

Before taking my stroll, I stepped to the edge. I unthinkingly looked down from the point from which I had first seen him. I cannot describe the chill that seized me. Near the mouth of the tunnel, I saw what appeared to be a man. His left sleeve was across his eyes. He was passionately waving his right arm.

The nameless horror that weighed me down passed in a moment. For in a moment, I saw that what appeared to be a man was a man indeed. There was a little group of other men standing a short distance from him. The man seemed to be repeating the gesture he'd made before.

The Danger light was not yet lighted. Against its pole was a little hut, that was entirely new to me. It was made of some wooden supports and tarpaulin.[4] It looked no bigger than a bed.

I had an awful sense that something was wrong. I felt a flash of guilty fear that something fatal had come of my leaving the man there. I had not sent anyone to oversee or correct what he did. I proceeded down the worn path with all the speed I could manage.

"What is the matter?" I asked the men.

"Signalman killed this morning, sir."

"Not the man belonging to that box?"

"Yes, sir."

"Not the man I know?"

"You will recognize him, sir, if you knew him," said the man who spoke for the others. He solemnly raised an end of the tarpaulin. "His face is quite intact."

[4]A tarpaulin is a large sheet of material such as waterproofed canvas. It is commonly called a tarp.

"Oh! How did this happen, how did this happen?" I asked. I turned from one to another as the hut was closed again.

"He was cut down by an engine, sir. No man in England knew his work better. But somehow he was not clear of the outer rail. It was just at broad daylight. He had put out the light and had the lamp in his hand. As the engine came out of the tunnel, his back was toward her. She cut him down. This man drove her—show the gentleman how it happened, Tom."

The man wore rough dark clothes. He stepped back to where he had been standing at the mouth of the tunnel.

"Coming around the curve in the tunnel, sir," he said, "I saw him at the end. It was like seeing him through a spyglass.⁵ There was no time to cut speed, and I knew him to be very careful. Since he didn't seem to take heed of the whistle, I shut it off. When we were running close to him, I called to him as loud as I could."

"What did you say?"

"I said, 'Below there! Look out! Look out! *For God's sake, clear the way!*'"

I was startled.

"Ah! It was a dreadful time, sir. I never stopped calling to him. I put this arm before my eyes so I would not see him. And I waved this arm to the last. But it was no use."

I do not wish to make the story any longer or dwell on any one of its curious events more than on any other. But I will, in closing, point out a coincidence.

The engine driver's warning included the words of the unlucky signalman. He had repeated them to me and said they haunted him. But the driver's warning also included my own words. He spoke the words that I myself—not the signalman—had given to the frantic gesture that the signalman had seen before. And I had said them only in my own mind.

⁵A spyglass is a small telescope.

INSIGHTS INTO
CHARLES DICKENS (1812–1870)

"The Signalman" is one story in the collection entitled *Mugby Junction*. These stories were not all written by Charles Dickens, and few of them deal with ghosts. They are all told from the perspective of the narrator, Barbox Brothers. He is a man who has spent much of his life in an office and has set out to see more of the world.

The *Mugby Junction* stories first appeared in a magazine. Most of Dickens' fiction was first published in magazines. They were published one chapter at a time, or *serialized*.

Dickens wrote several stories about ghosts. The most popular one is *A Christmas Carol,* which has been made into movies, television shows, and a play. But Dickens' fiction typically doesn't deal with the supernatural. He often wrote about the social problems of his time, such as poverty and the cruel treatment of orphans. He drew much of his material from his own difficult childhood.

Late in his life, Dickens gave many lectures and public appearances. He died when he was working on *The Mystery of Edwin Drood.* The "mystery" the title refers to is the hero, who disappears during the story. Unfortunately, Dickens never finished this novel. So people have been trying to figure out what happened to poor Edwin Drood ever since!

Other works by Charles Dickens:
A Christmas Carol, novel
David Copperfield, novel
Great Expectations, novel
Oliver Twist, novel